GROOMED FOR MURDER

ANNABELLE ARCHER WEDDING PLANNER COZ MYSTERY

LAI

BROADM⌣ ⋊⋉

CHAPTER 1

"Have you seen Cher?" Fern asked as he hurried up to me with a round brush in one hand and a can of industrial strength hair spray in the other.

I took a deep breath and got a whiff of the high-end hair products that had become the society hairstylist's signature scent. "I'm sorry. Did you ask me if I've seen Cher?"

Fern sighed. "Cher Noble. Our drag queen officiant."

You know you're busy when you almost forget you've hired a drag queen Cher impersonator to perform the wedding ceremony. I snapped my fingers. "Of course. How could I forget?"

Fern raised an eyebrow at me. My go-to hair guru usually looked impeccable on wedding days, but I noticed a strand of dark hair had escaped his low ponytail and dangled in his face. Then again, the day's humidity wasn't doing anyone's hair any favors. Luckily, my own long auburn hair was holding steady in a tight bun on the top of my head, but it had taken almost every bobby pin in my emergency kit to hold it in place.

I glanced down at the wedding day timeline with my "Wedding Belles" logo printed on top. "She should be on-site, but I haven't seen her yet."

Fern stepped aside to let a massive urn filled with garden flowers walk between us and flicked a bit of pollen off his gold lamé blazer when a lily brushed against him. If I didn't know the attendants were wearing gold sparkly dresses, I would have found his outfit out of place in the garden setting, but today's wedding was all about garden meets glam and, as usual, Fern's outfit—a shiny gold jacket with a large silk rose boutonniere—was on point. His ability and desire to coordinate with wedding decor never ceased to amaze me. I didn't have nearly his style—nor did I care nearly as much—so I stuck with classic black dresses on wedding days, while he'd been known to wear seersucker suits paired with bowties, Indian saris, and full kimonos.

Fern blew the errant strand of hair off his face. "If you see her, could you please tell her I'm in the vendor room with the groomsmaids?"

"Will do. We're not calling them bridesmaids?"

"We don't have a bride, now do we?"

He had a point. I suppose it didn't make sense to have brides-maids for a wedding with two grooms. I watched Fern rush back inside the Meridian House, and I returned to surveying the cere-mony setup in the garden.

Even though the day was typical for spring in Washington, DC —a little cool and threatening rain—we were going ahead with the outdoor plan. Two huge stone garden urns overflowing with flowers flanked a massive tree at the end of the grassy lawn, and white wooden folding chairs extended back from it in two even rows. At the back of the chairs we'd built a long wooden bar with smaller floral urns on each end and placed a massive silver bowl in the center filled with ice and several magnums of pink cham-pagne. Glass champagne coupes sat on silver trays ready to be filled and handed to guests once the ceremony ended.

I pivoted and looked into the linden tree grove where guests would walk after the ceremony ended and after they were handed a glass of pink bubbly. The branches of the tall spindly trees were beginning to bloom and create a canopy of green over the pebbled area extending off the back of the historic home. We'd suspended industrial-style pendant lights between the trees and had arranged modern white lounge furniture on the raised terrace behind the fountain. It was pretty now, but it would look magical once the sun had set and the lights lit the garden with a soft glow.

"Annabelle!" My assistant's voice drew my eyes to the large glass doors leading into the house from the linden grove. Kate stood at the top of the short flight of stone stairs descending into the garden, tapping one black high heel and flicking her blond bob away from her face.

I crossed the bed of small pebbles toward her since I knew it would take Kate twice as long to get to me in her absurdly high heels. I wore flats during setup for exactly this reason. "What's up?" I said once I'd reached her.

She handed me several bright-red gummy bears, which I knew was her way of softening me up. "The groom wants to add a short reading to the ceremony."

I popped the squishy candy into my mouth and enjoyed the rush of sweetness before answering her. "Now? The programs have already been printed."

She shrugged one shoulder. "That's what I told him."

"Which one is it?" I asked.

Kate took a packet of gummy bears from her dress pocket and shook a few into her palm. "Which reading is it?"

"No. Which groom is it?"

She raised an eyebrow at me. "Take a wild guess."

I didn't need to. Since we'd started planning Stefan's and Jesse's wedding six months ago, Stefan had been nothing but a high-maintenance diva. Working with him had made me regret complaining about bridezillas. Those girls were amateurs compared to this.

As the owner of Wedding Belles, the wedding planning company behind some of Washington DC's most elite society weddings, I'd seen my share of dramatic brides, difficult mothers, and attention-grabbing bridesmaids. I thought after seven years of weddings for the powerful and power hungry, I'd seen it all. I was wrong. Every decision had involved tears, ultimatums, and sometimes prescription medication. And that was just on the Wedding Belles side of things.

I put a finger to my left eye, which had begun to twitch since working with Groomzilla. "So who does Stefan want to do this reading?"

"He says it's fine if Cher Noble does it." Kate shoved the rest of the gummy bears into her mouth and wadded up the empty cellophane packet.

I took a pen out of the pocket of my dress and made a note in the margins of my schedule. "As soon as I see Cher, I'll be sure to tell her. I'm going to go out on a limb and guess Stefan does *not* have a copy of the reading with him."

Kate swallowed her mouthful. "You guess right. He says we can find it online. It's Supreme Court Justice Kennedy's final paragraph in his ruling on gay marriage."

I knew the passage since several of our same-sex couples had used it since the ruling. Luckily, it was short. "I'll write it out for Cher and tell her to stick it in at the end. Anything else?"

Kate studied me. "You really should get your eye checked out. Or maybe wear a patch."

I put a hand over my lid and could feel it fluttering. "You mean like a pirate? That wouldn't be distracting at all."

Kate tilted her head. "If you wore your hair down and flipped it over one side of your face you could pull it off. Although I do like your boss bun."

"I'm sure it will go away once this wedding is over," I said, lowering my voice as a waiter passed by with an armful of black-and-white chevron-patterned linens. "It's the Stefan effect."

"At least Jesse is a doll," Kate said, "although I've yet to figure out why he's marrying Stefan."

"Stefan is a power gay," Richard said as he came up behind Kate.

I dropped my hand from my eye and assessed Richard's tailored black suit, gunmetal-gray shirt and tie, and perfectly spiked brown hair. Even though he'd been in the kitchen for the past hour getting ready to cater the wedding, you'd never know it. Not a splatter on him. "Which is?"

"You know he's one of the partners of the restaurant company that owns all those trendy new places in New York. They opened one here last month."

"I knew he was in restaurants," I said.

Richard shot his eyes heavenward. "Annabelle, you have *got* to start Googling your clients. Anyway, Stefan is rich and stylish and au courant."

"If that's French for 'colossal jerk,' we're already well-aware," Kate said.

Richard arched a brow at her. "Stick to French kissing, darling."

Kate craned her neck behind her to look inside the house. "I would if there was anyone on-site worth kissing. Speaking of hotties, is the photographer here yet?"

"You mean the married photographer?" I asked.

Kate winked at me. "I only look. I never touch."

I knew firsthand that rule only applied to married men. The single ones were fair game, and she did plenty of touching. I followed her gaze, although I was not searching for the cute photographer. Through the glass doors I could see waiters carrying racks of glassware into the dining room and several burly men wearing all black and rolling dollies across the foyer. A pair of guys stood on ladders adjusting lighting, while a tall, thin man walked by with a guitar case.

Richard ignored Kate. "I don't know why you two are complaining. I'm the one who had to have three tastings with them. One of them only to taste sauces."

"I know," I said. "Kate and I were at every one of them."

"Stefan is such a pill but Jesse is so sweet." Kate stepped out of one of her heels and wiggled her toes. "I can't figure out why they're together."

Richard glanced behind him. "Word on the street is Stefan has a thing for buff guys."

"Jesse is that," Kate admitted. "And *he* must have a thing for tall, blond, and intimidating."

"Or he likes the prospect of being a kept man," Richard said. "Although, I don't know if I could put up with Stefan's moods."

"Be glad you didn't have to go with them to drag queen brunch to audition officiants," I told him.

"I kind of liked that part," Kate said.

"You liked the bottomless mimosas," I reminded her. "I'm surprised you remember much of the experience."

"I remember most of it," she mumbled.

Richard tapped his fingers on his arm. "How many times have I suggested you put a set number of meetings in your contract?"

I ignored him because he'd given me the same advice many times, and each time I'd brushed it off. I hated Richard being right as much as he reveled in it.

Kate held up both hands. "Can we all focus on being happy it's almost over?" She dropped her voice so only I could hear her. "And on Monday morning, you and I are changing our contract."

"On Monday morning, I'm sleeping in," I said.

Kate nudged me, her voice still a whisper. "Why? Is Reese sleeping over?"

"No. Maybe. I mean, I don't know." I felt my cheeks warm. Kate meant Mike Reese, DC police detective and my still-new boyfriend. After months of stops and starts, we'd finally been seeing each other steadily, although I didn't feel comfortable talking details. Especially not in front of Richard, who had been my best friend for years and who tended to get a bit jealous now he had to share me with Reese.

"What's this?" Richard asked.

"Nothing." I shot Kate a look as I pulled my phone out of my pocket to check the time. "We have one hour until early-bird guests may start to arrive." I turned to Richard. "Is the kitchen almost ready?"

Richard gave me a withering look. "When is my kitchen not ready? The doll who runs the house let me in an hour early."

Kate's eyes lit up. "Is Mary here yet?"

I held up a finger. "I love her too, but no socializing until we are completely ready." I flipped through my schedule where I'd checked off vendors as they'd arrived for setup. I could hear the band doing a sound check inside, so I didn't need to ask if they were ready. "So it looks like the only vendor not checked in is the officiant."

"Would she happen to be over six feet tall with shoulders like a linebacker, black hair down to her waist, and wearing a sequined cocktail dress?" Richard asked.

"That should be Cher Noble," I said. "I hope to God there aren't two people here who fit that description."

"It's a gay wedding, Annabelle," Richard said. "You never know. Anyway, I saw your drag queen du jour heading into the library about twenty minutes ago. She asked me if it was okay for her to rehearse in there."

I felt a momentary flutter of panic when I heard the word "rehearse." I'd seen Cher Noble's act on stage at drag queen brunch. If she was planning on putting on a similar show, we were in for an irreverent wedding ceremony. "Are you sure she didn't head into the room with the piano?"

He shook his head. "No, but both grooms have been in and out of that room putting things at their head table. I'm about to bar them from leaving the getting-ready room. You know how I feel about clients wandering around setup."

I knew Richard's thoughts on almost everything since he rarely had an unexpressed one.

Kate put a hand on my arm. "I'm sure Cher's going over the script Stefan gave her. Why don't we go check in with her and give her the additional reading?"

"I'll come with you." Richard produced a sheaf of papers from his inside jacket pocket. "I need to do a final pass of the tables and make sure the seating matches the floor plan."

Kate led the way through the marble-floored loggia and past the table displaying escort cards arranged in rows around a towering floral arrangement. A woman in gardening gloves stood next to the table pulling loose tulips from a collection of orange buckets at her feet, clipping the ends off the stems with floral clippers, inserting floral wire into them to keep them straight, and adding them to the urn. I glanced at the number of blooms left in the buckets and wondered if she could really fit them all in the container without it collapsing from the weight. We reached the large wooden double doors leading into the library, and Kate and I each took one antique brass handle and pulled hard.

The doors swung open to reveal a room with sage-green walls and built-in shelves filled with leather-bound books. Two tall arched windows on the opposite side of the door filled the room with light, although the ornate chandelier in the middle was turned off. Five round tables surrounded by ladder-backed reception chairs filled the room and were topped with lush arrangements of spring flowers, making the space smell like a garden.

"She's not here." Kate stepped inside and rested her hands on the back of a chair.

"Maybe she finished rehearsing." Richard stepped around us and began counting off chairs with his pointer finger.

"Fern was looking for her," I said, leaning over and adjusting one of the gold laser-cut table numbers protruding from a flower arrangement. "Maybe she's with him.

Richard paused as he reached the middle of the room, pressing a hand to his chest as he stared down at the floor. "She's right here."

"What?" I looked at Richard's stricken expression as Kate and I rushed over to him.

Kate clutched my arm as the figure of the drag queen came into view. She lay sprawled faceup on the parquet floor, her long dark hair fanned out around the shoulders of her royal-blue sequined dress and a hot-pink feather boa wrapped tightly around her neck. From the purple tinge of her face and the placement of the boa, it looked like Cher Noble had been strangled.

Richard shook his head. "And with her own boa no less."

I looked away so I wouldn't be sick and pressed my fingers over my eye as it began to twitch furiously.

CHAPTER 2

"**W**ho could have done this?" Kate asked as she backed away from the dead body.

I stole a look at the sequined corpse and looked away quickly. Cher's long black wig had gotten skewed in the attack or the fall, and the center part was now over her right eye. I wasn't sure if it was the artificial arch of her eyebrows, but her expression was one of surprise. I wondered if she'd known the person who did this to her. Or was she so shocked because she didn't? I felt a wave of nausea and closed my eyes for a moment, taking a deep breath to keep from throwing up the gummy bears I'd recently eaten.

"Who would kill a drag queen wedding officiant?" I whispered as I opened my eyes again and stepped away from the body to stand next to Kate. Oddly enough, the drag queen's perfume smelled more like Old Spice than Chanel, and the fragrance did not mix well with the scent of fresh flowers. I tried not to think of the other smells that would soon fill the room.

"And why on a wedding day?" Richard rubbed his arms. "It's been a madhouse in here."

"Maybe that makes it the perfect time," Kate said. "I know I couldn't tell you all the people who've been in and out of the house all day."

I put a hand to my forehead. "It doesn't matter who did it or why right now. What matters is we have a dead body lying in the exact place people are supposed to eat dinner in a couple of hours."

Richard staggered backward. "This means my lobster medallions are going to be served rubbery, doesn't it? Could this day get any worse?"

I reminded myself Richard's reaction was normal for a culinary person obsessed with perfect food. Or a sociopath.

Kate fumbled for her phone. "Should I call 911?"

I shook my head. "If we call the cops, our wedding is going to be one giant crime scene. And Stefan is going to blame us."

Kate bit her bottom lip. "He can't blame us for a murder. It's not like we killed Cher Noble. We didn't even suggest hiring a drag queen to officiate the ceremony."

"Do you think that will matter to him?" I glanced at the closed library doors. "You know the buck always stops with us. No matter what." I shook my head. "We need to fix this."

Richard folded his arms over his chest. "How do you intend to fix a dead drag queen? I refuse to be involved in any sort of *Weekend at Bernie's* nonsense."

I tapped my chin with one finger. "Nothing like that. I've learned my lesson about trying to hide dead bodies." I hated to admit this wasn't the first time we'd stumbled across a murder victim at a wedding, and not all my attempts to "keep calm and carry on" had worked out so well. But it was my wedding planner instinct to fix any problem and make sure my couple had a magical wedding day, even if it meant not calling the cops at the first sign of trouble.

"Have you?" Richard asked, giving me a pointed look. "I seem to recall a wedding on a yacht where you didn't think it was such a bad idea."

I leveled a finger at my best friend. "Hey, buddy. I didn't hear you complaining when you got to make it through cocktail hour without your food being overcooked or served cold."

Richard turned away from me in a huff. "I almost ended up on the evening news wearing a trash bag, Annabelle." He took out a gray-and-white-striped handkerchief and began fanning his face. "Me! With a Hefty bag duck taped around myself." He pressed the silk square to his lips to stifle a sob. "You couldn't even tell I was wearing Prada underneath."

Kate held up her hands. "Okay, okay. I'm with Richard. Keeping things from the cops hasn't always turned out so well for us. I also agree with Annabelle. Our client is not going to be even remotely sympathetic about this. We're between a rock and a hard face."

I paused for a moment while I thought that Kate's mangled expression wasn't so far off, although I wasn't quite sure who she considered the hard face. I heard the band warming up across the foyer and the clinking of glasses being set out in the adjoining room. I could even hear the faint noise of a leaf blower as the linden grove was cleared of fallen leaves. We still had a little less than an hour until guests showed up, an hour and a half until ceremony start, and two hours until reception time. Not long enough to get the cops in and out, that was for sure. But maybe we had enough time to move the wedding entirely.

"You know the house next door?" I asked. "White-Meyer?"

"It's all owned by the same management company," Richard said.

"And the gardens connect through the brick arch on the side," Kate said. "The houses even share the same alley for loading."

"And White-Meyer never has a big event when Meridian has a wedding going on," I reminded them. "So the house should be empty."

Richard's mouth fell open. "Are you suggesting we move the

entire wedding next door?" He glanced at his Gucci watch. "In less than an hour?"

I motioned to the dead body. "Would you rather have your waiters step over Cher as they serve the soup course?"

Kate shuddered and turned her body away from the corpse. "Don't even joke."

"We can't do this without asking the house first," Richard said. "You're out of your mind if you think I'm going to get banned for life because I co-opted a historic house without permission."

"Of course we're going to ask," I said. I hadn't figured out exactly how I would word my request so it seemed like the most logical solution. Since the events director, Mary, had met Stefan, she knew the level of crazy we were dealing with.

Richard squared his shoulders. "Let me handle it. She'll understand once I explain everything. Anyway, Mary and I have bonded over our love of dogs."

"I beg your pardon, what?" I asked. "Your love of . . .?"

Richard sighed. "Mary loves Hermes. And I brought by some of my homemade dog biscuits for her little beagles last week."

For as long as I'd known Richard, he'd had a hard-and-fast rule about children and dogs. Both were too loud and messy for his designer lifestyle. But a tiny Yorkie named Butterscotch had been part of the package when Richard had started dating PJ. Even though I hadn't met the boyfriend yet, I'd become acquainted with his dog when Richard began carrying the pup around in his man bag. He'd even renamed the dog Hermes, a name he claimed better suited the upscale pooch and him.

"You and Mary talk about your dogs?" Kate asked, looking at Richard as if he'd sprouted antennae.

Richard gave her an arch look. "I'll have you know, she values my opinion on where to buy the best doggie sweaters."

"And I thought the dead drag queen was the weirdest part of this day," Kate said under her breath.

I put a hand on Richard's arm. "You go talk to Mary. Explain everything. Beg, plead, remind her about Stefan."

"On it." Richard spun on his heel and slipped out one of the double doors, pulling it closed behind him.

Kate stepped further away from the dead body, resting her hand on one of the brass doorknobs. "What do *we* do?"

I pulled out my cell phone. "I'm going to call Reese."

"What about the whole 'cops will ruin the wedding' thing?" She held her fingers up to make air quotes.

I found his number in my recent call log. "I'm hoping if I explain my completely legal plan that doesn't touch his crime scene, he'll cut me some slack."

Kate elbowed me. "The only reason he'd go along with this is if you're giving him a good reason. Are you giving him a good reason? Or are you planning to tonight?"

I felt my face warm. "If you're implying the only reason he would go along with my plan is because we're . . . "

"Doing the horizontal mambo?" Kate said, finishing my sentence in a way I never would have.

I smacked her arm. "I never told you that."

"No, you haven't." Kate let out a breath. "And it's driving me crazy. Come on, I tell you about my love life. Quid pro quo."

"I know you have," I said. "And I'm scarred for life. I can never unhear some of those stories."

Kate grinned. "I really should write a book, shouldn't I?"

I couldn't even imagine where such a book would be shelved. I shook my head as I speed dialed Reese. "While I'm talking to him, I need you to find a backup officiant and break the news to Fern."

"And should I meet you back here?" she asked, her eyes flitting to the body in the middle of the room. "You're going to stay in here?"

I gave a jerk of my head as the phone rang. "To make sure no one disturbs the scene."

Kate grimaced as she slid out of the room. When she pulled

the door shut behind her, the only sound was the ringing of the phone in my ear. Just as I was convinced it would go to voicemail, Reese answered.

"Hey, babe. I thought you were working all day."

Hearing his deep voice made me smile, even if I wasn't happy about the reason for my call. "I am. I ran into a little snafu."

"Uh oh. Your idea of a little snafu usually involves a full-scale police investigation."

"Speaking of the police, are you on duty today?" I tried to make my voice sound casual, but I knew it was higher pitched than usual.

"Yes." He drew the word out as he said it. "Why do I have a bad feeling about this?"

"What if I asked you to be discreet about something?"

"Annabelle," his voice was serious. "What's going on?"

"Cher Noble, the drag queen officiant for today's wedding, was strangled with her boa."

A long silence followed by a groan.

I took a breath and barreled on. "But if I postpone the wedding, the groom will probably sue me, so we're leaving the body untouched. The wedding will now be held in the historic house next door. That way your crime scene is preserved and so is my career."

"Where are you?"

"Meridian International Center in DC," I said. "But can you not use the sirens? The neighbors here are a bit touchy."

"They're really not going to like the rest of the day," he muttered. "I have to call in the medical examiner and an ambulance."

"Okay, but can you ask everyone to be discreet? I really want to keep the situation as low-key as possible."

Both doors behind me flung open, and I spun around to see Fern standing wild-eyed in front of me. "Where is she?"

I tried to block him from pushing past me. "You can't mess up the crime scene. The police are on their way."

Kate ran up behind Fern. "I tried to stop him, but he didn't take the news so well."

"Cher!" Fern cried as he spotted the dead drag queen. "We've got to get the boa off her. She can't breathe."

I wrapped both arms around Fern to keep him from lunging at the body. Kate grabbed him from behind, and we pushed him out of the room.

"She's dead," I told him once he'd stopped straining against me. "There's nothing you can do to help her."

Fern's wide eyes focused on me before he let out a blood-curdling scream. "Someone here is a murderer!"

The band stopped playing, the waiters stopped setting up, and Kate and I froze as everyone turned to look at us. I caught Fern as he slumped against me in a dead faint.

So much for keeping things low-key.

CHAPTER 3

"**W**ell, that wasn't pretty," Richard said as he walked up to me.

I stood at the top of the double staircases leading from the ground level up to the main floor of Meridian House. I had a good view of the front entrance below, the closed doors to the library, and a straight line of sight to the outside garden. Instead of the sounds of the band rehearsing, I heard the clattering of cases as they packed up to move next door. Glasses clinked in the dining room as waiters filled racks and carried them outside and through the brick archway to the historic home next door.

"You mean Fern's reaction to seeing Cher Noble?" I gave him a look. "Might I remind you you've been known to swoon before?"

Richard waved a hand at me. "Not that, and for heaven's sake, stop using the word swoon. It makes me sound like a character in a Regency romance. I meant it wasn't pretty watching my guys walk the ceremony bar across the linden grove to the White-Meyer house."

I peered around him to look outside and held my breath as three tuxedo-clad waiters gently lifted the towering stack of cheese wheels doing double duty as the wedding cake and began shuffling it through the loggia. "Did it make it in one piece?"

"Barely, but yes. Buster and Mack are moving the floral urns, and then my waiters will start switching the chairs."

I noticed the overflowing urn of tulips had already disappeared from the escort card table, and only the empty orange buckets and florist supplies remained in the corner of the room as evidence of the décor. I still needed to gather up the cards with guests' names and reposition them next door, but I knew I still had time.

I pulled my phone out of my dress pocket and noted the time. "We should make it. Kate's outside repositioning the valets and having one stand in front of Meridian to redirect any stragglers."

"I hate to mention this, darling." Richard shifted from one foot to the other. "When I was outside, it was spitting a bit."

"Spitting? As in rain?" I shook my head. "Nope. The forecast didn't call for rain until later tonight after our ceremony and cocktails are long over."

"Okay . . ." Richard drew the word out to several syllables.

"Absolutely not." I crossed my arms in front of my chest. "I have to deal with a groom from hell and a dead body? I refuse to be rained out as well."

Richard touched a hand to my shoulder. "Are you feeling all right? You look a bit manic and your eye . . ." He pointed to my twitching eyelid.

I put a hand over it. "I'm totally fine. Why is everyone obsessed with my eye?"

"Maybe because it looks like it's about to twitch off your face," Richard mumbled, putting an arm around my shoulder. "Are you sure we're okay to do all this?" His eyes darted to the entrance of the historic house as if a SWAT team might burst in at any second.

"We aren't touching anything remotely near the murder scene," I said with more confidence than I felt. I had suspected relocating a wedding after finding a dead body might not be exactly kosher with the DC police, but I'd always found it was better to ask forgiveness than permission. Something I'd learned from Richard and seemed to do a lot of with Detective Reese. "No one has gone near the library since we dragged Fern out."

A chef in a white jacket passed us carrying two large silver trays, and I got a whiff of bacon. No doubt Richard's brown sugar bacon-wrapped scallops. My stomach growled, virtually empty save for the few gummy bears I'd eaten earlier.

Richard shook his head. "You had to know he would be upset."

"How? No one told me they were friends." I nibbled on the edge of my thumbnail, and Richard swatted it out of my mouth. "Is he okay?"

Richard bobbled his head back and forth. "He's over in the other house with the grooms and their attendants. He seemed to calm down once he had some champagne."

"You gave him booze?" I rolled my eyes. No one loved bubbly as much as Fern, but it usually made him louder and more dramatic, and he was already plenty of both to start with.

"I stocked the new getting-ready room with plenty of champagne and a tray of the grooms' favorite hors d'oeuvres. They're all drinking, so no one will notice if Fern gets a bit tipsy."

I squeezed Richard's arm. "Good thinking on the hors d'oeuvres. Stefan loves your mushroom chopsticks. Maybe he'll eat so many he'll forget to be outraged. How did he take it when you told him about Cher Noble?"

"Surprisingly well." Richard didn't meet my eyes. "Especially since I told him we were moving because of a broken AC unit and not because their drag queen officiant had been murdered."

"What?" I gaped at him. "You didn't tell the grooms their officiant is dead?"

"You told me to move them to the house next door and keep them happy, which I did. If I told them Cher had been killed, they would not be nearly so happy."

"How are we going to explain why the person marrying them

isn't a six-foot-five drag queen dressed like Cher from the 'If I Could Turn Back Time Farewell Tour?'" I tapped my foot on the wooden floor. "I think they're going to notice."

"Kate wasn't able to get another Cher impersonator to do the ceremony?"

I narrowed my eyes at him. "Do you know how many drag queen Cher impersonators are licensed by the District of Columbia to perform legal wedding ceremonies?" I didn't wait for an answer. "One. The only officiant Kate could find who could get over here on a busy Saturday during high wedding season was a rabbi. At least this rabbi is 'Jewish light,' so he'll do the ceremony before sundown."

Now it was Richard's turn to gape at me. "A rabbi? You must be out of your mind. The couple isn't even Jewish."

"Don't you think I know that?" I tried to keep my voice from reaching howler-monkey volume. "We didn't exactly have a lot to choose from. Kate even called Perry's restaurant where we found Cher, but there's some big drag show out of state so all the drag queens are in New Jersey."

"There's a scary thought." Richard ran a hand through his choppy bangs. "Is there any chance the rabbi will wear a Cher wig and a cocktail dress? I think I could scrape those up and get them over here in time."

I didn't ask how he could pull it off because I really didn't want to know. "I'm pretty sure eighty-year-old Rabbi Hoffman is going to say no."

"Nobody goes the extra mile anymore." Richard shook his head. "Don't even get me started on finding decent wait staff."

I heard the jingling of metal and looked up to see Buster and Mack, our two floral designers, rushing across the emptied-out loggia toward us. The two men each topped six feet and three hundred pounds and wore lots of black leather biker garb with metal rivets and chains, which meant I could always hear them coming if I didn't feel the ground trembling first. They were known as much for their custom Harleys as they were for their lush, modern floral designs.

"All the floral from outside has been transitioned over," Mack said, rubbing a hand over his dark-red goatee. "Can we start on the inside arrangements?"

"Do the large standing pieces we had flanking the band first," I said. "Let's leave the table arrangements for last."

Buster cleared his throat, but his voice still came out as a gravelly rumble. "The back terrace next door is nothing compared to the linden grove. Are you sure the AC can't be fixed in time?"

I shot Richard a look. "You told everyone it was an AC problem?"

"You know how wedding people talk," Richard said. "I didn't want it to get back to Stefan."

Mack looked from me to Richard. "It isn't an issue with the AC?"

I touched a hand to Mack's thick forearm. "Actually, the officiant's been murdered."

Mack sucked in air and clamped a hand over his mouth.

"But we just saw the rabbi wandering out behind White-Meyer house," Buster said. "When did he get killed?"

"Not the rabbi," Richard said. "He's the new officiant. The original officiant is the one who was killed. Cher Noble."

Buster's left eyebrow raised slightly, and the black motorcycle goggles on the top of his head followed. "At least that explains why we don't have a chuppah for the ceremony. I saw the rabbi and started to worry we'd missed something on the proposal."

Mack took Buster's hand. "We should say a prayer for Miss Noble."

Buster and Mack were part of a Christian biker gang and included all of us on their weekly prayer chain. Before I could tell Mack we didn't have time for a prayer vigil, the entrance doors to the house swung open below us, and Detective Mike Reese stepped inside, followed by a pair of paramedics carrying bright-orange duffel bags.

Reese wore black pants and a gray shirt with the sleeves rolled up to his elbows. I felt my stomach flutter as he moved his sunglasses to the top of his head and looked up at me, a dark curl falling onto his forehead.

"Looks like someone's prayers were answered." Mack elbowed me as the handsome detective began walking up the steps toward us.

"That's my cue to go find the rabbi," Richard said. "The last thing we need is to lose another officiant. And maybe I can talk him into the wig while I'm at it."

I started to tell Richard not to scare off our only chance at a legal wedding ceremony, but he'd already spun on his heels and left. I would have to talk to him about his jealousy issues as soon as I dealt with this wedding crisis.

When Reese got to the top of the landing, he leaned down and gave me a quick kiss on the cheek. "You okay?" he asked, resting a hand on the small of my back.

"I'm fine." I gave him as much of a smile as I could muster.

He shook Buster's and Mack's hands while I tried to ignore both men's giddy expressions. Apparently my dating life had been on their prayer list for a long time, and they took shared credit—along with the Almighty and the other bikers on their prayer chain—for the fact I now had a hot boyfriend.

"Where's the body?" Reese asked.

I pointed to the closed library doors and watched while he led the paramedics and another man I assumed was a plainclothes detective to the crime scene. They left the doors open, but I didn't try to watch. I knew Cher was dead, and seeing the paramedics work on her was not a visual I wanted to add to the day's memories.

"How was she killed?" Mack whispered to me as blue uniformed officers filed into the house and up the stairs.

"Strangled," I said. "With her own boa."

Buster shook his head. "Who would want to kill a wedding officiant?"

Mack's eyes widened. "You don't think we're all in danger, do you? The killer could still be on-site."

I doubted someone would kill a person and stick around. Unless they were involved in the set-up—an unsettling thought. "I don't think it has anything to do with the wedding. None of the other vendors knew Cher, and the schedule I sent out to the team didn't have her name on it. I don't usually put the officiant on the vendor list."

"We had no idea who was performing the ceremony," Buster said. "Not that we need to."

"So no one here would have known the victim would be here," Mack said.

"Well, not no one." I turned my body so I faced away from the activity in the library. "Kate and I both knew since we went with the couple to help pick her out. Richard knew because it came up during our three tastings, and Fern also knew."

"How did Fern know?" Mack asked. "Does he normally get involved with the ceremony?"

"Never." I tapped my chin as I tried to remember how Fern had known about Cher Noble. "But apparently Fern was also friends with the victim. He was pretty hysterical when he found out she'd been killed."

"So the only individual here with a personal connection to the victim was your friend Fern?" Reese's voice made me jump.

When I turned around and saw him with his notebook out, my mouth went dry. Had I implicated one of my best friends in a murder?

CHAPTER 4

"You're going to have to tell Fern," Kate said as we crossed under the brick archway leading from the linden grove to the house next door.

I spotted the band's white box truck idling in the alley between the houses as empty cases were loaded on. I breathed in the exhaust fumes and coughed. "Tell him what?"

"Oh, I don't know. That you let slip to your boyfriend he was connected to the victim, and now he's a person of interest in the case."

I held up a finger. "First of all, the information Fern and Cher Noble were friends would have come out eventually. And second, Reese doesn't think he has anything to do with the murder. He thinks Fern might have some special insight into the victim and why she might have been killed."

"You keep telling that to yourself." Kate held up a glass vial. "In case Fern doesn't see it your way, I brought the smelling salts."

I heard the crystals rattling against the glass as she shook it. "Smelling salts? Seriously?"

"Don't knock the smelling salts. They came in handy when the bridesmaid passed out in the church, and when the mother of the bride had an episode and didn't want to walk down the aisle."

Over the years, we'd added items to our emergency kits until they contained almost everything you could possibly need on a wedding day. Kate's kit contained a few items mine didn't, namely smelling salts and Valium. To be fair, both had been used more than once to great effect.

We reached the paved back terrace of the White-Meyer house, and I scanned the new ceremony setting created by the folding chairs and repositioned floral urns. Unfortunately, this house didn't have an expansive lawn or towering tree to add to the garden feel—only beige paving stones overlooking the tops of houses—so the decor appeared sparse.

I pulled out my phone. "Do you think Dale could get some trees over here in time if I called him?"

"I don't know," Kate said. "It's a Saturday in the spring. I'm sure our plant guy is busy installing palms and ficus trees all over the city."

I dropped my phone back into my dress pocket. "You're right. I guess our biggest problem isn't the ceremony backdrop lacking in greenery."

"I'd say the police investigation next door is a slightly bigger issue." Kate paused and stepped out of one of her heels, dropping her height down a few inches. "By the way, does your cop boy toy know we've moved the entire wedding next door and plan to go ahead with it?"

I swatted her arm and looked behind me to make sure no one had heard. "He's not my boy toy."

"You seemed uncomfortable with the word boyfriend, so I thought I'd try out some others."

"Boyfriend is better," I said. I hated to think of Reese's smug smile if he heard himself referred to as my boy toy.

"Fine. Does your boyfriend know about our switcheroo scheme?"

"I told him the wedding was next door. I may not have mentioned it wasn't always next door."

Kate raised one eyebrow. "Or we moved everything over?"

"Or that part," I said.

"Excellent." Kate held onto my arm as she slipped her foot back inside her high heel. "I look forward to the evening's fireworks when he finds out."

"There won't be fireworks this time, because I have no intention of getting involved in this case," I said.

"When have I heard that before?" Richard strode toward us from the back doors of the historic home.

"I may have gotten overzealous in the past, but this time I'm serious," I said once Richard reached us. "My days of poking around in criminal investigations are over."

Richard and Kate both stared at me without saying anything. It was true we'd had a surprising bit of bad luck when it came to dead bodies turning up at our weddings. It could also be argued I had a habit of getting sucked into the ensuing investigations, and I'd sucked my friends in right along with me.

I held up my palms in a gesture of surrender. "This time I promise. Anyway, if I did get involved, Reese would never talk to me again, which would make dating him a lot harder."

Kate tapped a finger against her chin. "But not impossible. I could go a long time 'not talking' to someone as hot as Reese."

Richard rolled his eyes. "Forget about the police for a second. We have a wedding starting in thirty minutes, and I had no luck with the rabbi."

I looked down and noticed he held a black wig in his hands. "That didn't come from Cher Noble did it?"

Richard gasped. "Are you suggesting I snatched a murdered drag queen bald-headed while she lay dead on the floor?"

I paused for a moment. "Did you?"

"No." Richard put a hand to his heart before lowering his voice. "I couldn't. Too many cops."

Kate eyed him. "Then where did you get the wig?"

"Do you really want to know the answer?" Richard asked.

I held up a hand. "I, for one, am fine not knowing."

Richard smoothed the long black hair of the wig. "It doesn't matter. Rabbi No-Fun refused to wear it."

He pointed to a small man in a blue suit standing between the two large urns of flowers and arranging items on the round ceremony table between them.

I put my fingers to my twitching eyelid as I watched Rabbi Hoffman set out the kiddush cup and the glass for the couple to break at the end of the ceremony. I twisted to face Kate. "Did you tell him the couple was Jewish?"

Kate bit her lower lip. "I didn't say they *weren't* Jewish."

"This should go over well," Richard said.

Even if our balding rabbi decided to don a Cher wig, I felt confident our grooms would notice part of their ceremony was in Hebrew.

"Hey, you said find a legal officiant." She waved a hand in the rabbi's direction. "Voila."

"It doesn't matter," I said with more confidence than I felt. "At least we have someone to perform the ceremony. The important thing is our grooms get married today."

"Speaking of grooms, shouldn't we check in with ours?" Kate asked. "If the champagne isn't doing the trick, I've got backup methods."

Richard glanced at Kate's glass vial. "Your smelling salts?"

She patted her dress pocket. "And Valium. We crush a few of these babies into their bubbly and they won't notice if the pope marries them."

"Let's hold off on drugging our clients unless it's absolutely necessary," I said. "Let's call the Valium the last resort plan."

"Suit yourself," Kate said. "But I think we're fast approaching last resort territory."

As we walked into the back doors of the White-Meyer house

and crossed through the library, I had to admit Kate was right. So far, this was far from a smooth wedding day. I shouldn't have been surprised. The more high-maintenance and micromanaging the client, the greater the chances of disaster. It never failed.

I took a breath to steel myself as Richard opened the tall wooden doors leading into the side dining room where he'd stashed the wedding party and Fern. For a quick solution, Richard had done an impressive job. A rectangular table draped in a black-and-white wedding linen, topped with silver champagne buckets and trays of hors d'oeuvres, stood at one end of the room. Light poured in from the many floor-to-ceiling windows throughout the room, and Fern stood by one as he styled the hair of a blond woman in a shimmery gold cocktail dress. Other women—equally blond and all wearing various shades and lengths of gold—sat around a few cocktail tables with two tuxedo-clad men.

"We're almost ready," Fern called out when he saw us. "Don't these tramps look flabulous?"

"Does he mean fabulous or is that a new hip word I don't know?" I whispered to Kate.

"I think he's drunk," Richard said under his breath. "Which is an improvement over sobbing and wailing, so I'll take it."

I eyed Fern's red-rimmed eyes and the empty champagne flute on the table next to him. I made a quick scan of the room, but no one else appeared to be drunk. Then, again, no one else knew about the dead officiant.

Stefan stood and walked over to us. He was tall, blond, and tanner than anyone should be in early spring in Washington, which made his ice-blue eyes look even more striking. He was too Nordic for my taste. I preferred his slightly shorter, broader, and dark-haired partner, Jesse, who had warm brown eyes, naturally bronze skin, and was a thousand percent less terrifying. Jesse gave me a finger wave from where he sat.

"I am *not* happy about this change, Annabelle." Stefan folded his arms tightly across his chest.

"I understand completely," I said. Validating my brides and grooms was key to their happiness. I'd learned that early on in my career as a wedding planner. "If there was any way to avoid it, you know I would have."

"Are we going to be behind schedule?" he asked, only slightly mollified.

"We've managed to move everything over, so we should be able to start the ceremony right on time." I watched as Richard walked over to the champagne buckets and pulled out the empty bottles. It looked like they were all empty, which was either a good thing or a bad thing.

"I hope Meridian doesn't expect me to pay for this." Stefan waved his arms in the air. "This is not what we contracted for."

"True," I said, "but some things are out of the house's control, and Mary was flexible in letting us take over White-Meyer house on short notice."

"Because their air conditioning broke," Stefan said. "That's not our fault."

I shot Richard a look as he backed out of the room with his arms full of empty champagne bottles. "About that . . ."

Jesse jumped up from the table. "Is it fixed?"

"Not exactly," I said. "It was actually never broken. Richard wanted to spare you the truth, but in light of everything, I think you need to know."

Fern gave a cross between a sob and a hiccup, and both men looked at him before turning back at me.

Kate elbowed me. "Rip off the Band-Aid, Annabelle."

"The reason we had to move houses isn't because of broken AC. There was a murder, and Meridian House is now an active crime scene."

Jesse's hand flew to his face as he sucked his breath in sharply, while Stefan blinked hard a few times. I ignored Fern's soft crying and the groomsmaids' shocked murmurs.

"Who was murdered?" Stefan asked.

"Cher Noble," I said. "Your officiant."

Jesse shook his head. "This is horrible. Poor Cher."

"So who's going to perform our ceremony?" Stefan asked while his fiancé looked slack-jawed at him.

I managed a weak smile but could feel my cheeks shaking from the strain of the manufactured expression. "We did find a replacement, but we were not able to locate another drag queen licensed to perform marriage ceremonies."

Jesse reached out and squeezed my arm. "I'm sure it will be fine. Thank you for finding someone so quickly, although I'm not sure if we should even go ahead with the ceremony at this point."

Stefan cut his eyes to him. "Of course we're going through with it. We have one hundred and fifty guests on their way, and we will not disappoint them."

Jesse opened his mouth as if to protest then seemed to think better of it.

Stefan turned to me. "I am not happy about this turn of events."

"Neither is Cher Noble," muttered Kate, who had less patience for Stefan than I did.

"Clearly, this is not ideal," I said, "but we're working with the police to keep your wedding as unaffected as possible."

"If it wasn't for Annabelle's connections, you'd all be in the middle of police interrogations right about now," Kate said. "I don't think you'd like us to tell all your society guests you've been taken down to the police station would you?"

Stefan's eyes widened for a moment. "Obviously we're grateful that's not happening."

The door behind us opened, and Reese's head appeared. "Can I talk to you?"

"That's the detective on the case," I said. "I'll be right back."

Kate pulled a pair of yarmulkes out of her dress pocket and slapped them in Stefan's hand. "Here. You and Jesse are going to need to wear these for the ceremony."

Both grooms gawked at the black beanies as Kate and I turned around and slipped out of the room.

"Is everything okay?" I asked once I'd pulled the wooden door closed.

Reese cocked an eyebrow at me.

"She means aside from the murder," Kate said.

"I'm going to need to talk to Fern," Reese said. "Especially if he's the only person who knew the deceased."

I glanced toward the doors. "Any chance we could wait until after the ceremony?"

Reese looked at me.

"Maybe until we get the grooms down the aisle?" Kate asked.

Reese let out a long breath. "We have a victim who has been violently murdered. A murder trumps your wedding ceremony."

"I know, I know." I let my shoulders slump. "I can't imagine who could have gotten mad enough at our officiant to strangle her. If she'd already done the ceremony and messed up, I would have said our groomzilla could have done it, but he would never do anything to ruin the wedding he's spent so long planning."

"And I don't think strangling with a feather boa is his style," Kate said. "Stefan would definitely shoot someone."

"I have news for you." Reese pointed a finger at Kate and then me. "This is not to be shared with anyone else, but the victim wasn't strangled with her boa."

"What?" Kate looked fixedly at him. "Why was her face purple and her eyes bugged out and bloodshot?"

"Oh, she was choked alright, but not with a boa. Her neck had much deeper cuts than a bunch of feathers could make. Whoever killed her used wire."

"Wire?" My mouth went dry. "Like a garrote?"

Reese moved his head slowly up and down. "Like a premeditated hit."

CHAPTER 5

"Right this way," I said to an arriving cluster of guests, sweeping a hand in the direction of the back terrace. I turned to Kate once they'd passed out of earshot. "Is the string quartet ready?"

She gave me two thumbs up. "I went over the cues with them."

I listened to the sounds of the ensemble as the notes drifted back to us. "Do I hear instrumental Madonna?"

Kate cocked her head to one side. "Sounds like it. This is Stefan's version of sacred music."

"Who knew 'Holiday' would sound so pretty on violins?" I let out a quick breath and glanced down at my timeline, checking off the last line item before the processional, and taking a peek at my phone. It was time.

"I know you don't want to hear this," Kate said, "but I felt some raindrops when I was outside."

I willed my eye not to start twitching. If this wedding got rained out after having its officiant murdered and being moved to another location, Stefan would lose his mind, and I would need to enter the witness relocation program.

"We have the parasols set out at the back of the aisle, right?" I asked.

"Yes, but those are for sun and they're paper. If it starts raining, I'm not sure how long they'll hold up."

"It won't start raining until after the ceremony," I said with more conviction than I felt.

"I hope you're right, boss."

"Me too." I cast my eyes to the closed doors behind which the grooms and their groomsmaids were waiting. "Ready to line them up?"

Kate produced her timeline from the pocket of her dress. "Are we keeping the order the same, or are we changing it around so it's more like a Jewish processional?"

I patted her arm. "Let's keep it the same since the grooms aren't actually Jewish. Why don't you line everyone up while I make sure the rabbi is in place?"

Kate headed for the holding room, and I headed for the back of the house, pausing when I saw Rabbi Hoffman standing at the doors leading out to the terrace. He was shorter than me and had thinning gray hair underneath his black satin yarmulke and a pair of wire rim glasses sliding down his nose. He held a black leather portfolio under his arm.

When he saw me, he pushed his glasses up and looked at his wristwatch. "I hope we're going to be on time. I do have another ceremony after this one."

"We're ready to go if you are," I said. I let my eyes drift past him to where guests were seated on rows of wooden folding chairs and saw only a handful of open chairs in the back. "Did Kate explain we'd like the simplest version of the ceremony?"

"I assume the bride and groom won't be circling each other at the beginning?"

My stomach tightened. "Correct, but did Kate not explain what kind of wedding this is?"

Rabbi Hoffman opened the leather portfolio. "I'm sure she did.

33

Let me look at my notes. It's a busy wedding day, you know. I've already performed two ceremonies today, and I have one more after this."

Four weddings on one day? Maybe I should have been a wedding officiant instead of a wedding planner.

I turned as I heard the sound of Kate's heels and Fern's hiccups behind me. Kate led the procession with Stefan behind her, followed by the four groomsmaids in their sparkly gold dresses and, finally, Jesse. Fern flitted between the women, touching up their hair with his round brush and his can of hairspray. In his shiny gold jacket, he almost looked like one of the bridal party, which was entirely his intention. I coughed as a cloud of spray drifted over.

"Let's do this," I said.

Kate left the front of the line and leaned her head out of the door, waving to the string quartet and giving them a nod. The song they were playing tapered off and a solo violin began the first few notes of "Like A Prayer."

"You can go," I whispered to the rabbi, stepping back so I was hidden behind the doorframe. I waved the rest of the processional forward.

Stefan gave me a tight smile as he waited with me in the doorway. He looked up and squinted. "Are those rain clouds?"

"It's not going to rain until after the ceremony," I said.

He raised a perfectly arched eyebrow at me. "Agreed."

I spotted the rabbi in place between the two urns of colorful flowers and touched Stefan's arm. "It's your turn."

He walked briskly down the aisle, twice as fast as we'd practiced in rehearsal, and I realized he must be more nervous than he let on. One of the groomsmaids stepped up, and I adjusted her bouquet so she wasn't holding it up under her chin. "Rest your forearms on your hip bones and walk slowly."

I sent her down the aisle and twisted around to see Detective Reese walk into the back of the room accompanied by a uniformed police officer. I told Kate to take over processional duty and hurried over to Reese. "I thought you were going to let us get through the ceremony."

"I am." He pointed to Fern fluttering around the attendants. "But you won't need him once you get the bridal party down the aisle will you?"

I heard Fern hiccup several times in quick succession. "No. He should have at least ten minutes before they come back down the aisle."

Another groomsmaid began her walk and the entire line moved up, including Fern, who now seemed to be trying to feather the sides of Jesse's hair.

"Are you sure you don't want to wait until Fern's had a chance to sober up?" I asked.

"When will that be?" Reese crossed his arms over his chest. "Wednesday?"

I heard the music change; it took me a few moments to recognize the theme song from *Game of Thrones* and remember it was Stefan and Jesse's favorite show.

"Don't be ridiculous," I said. "Fern is willing and able to talk to you, although I doubt he knows anything."

Kate walked up, brushing her hands together to signal the job was done. "The hard part is over. They're all down the aisle."

Reese pointed to the doorway behind us. "Including Fern."

Kate and I spun around in time to see Fern snatch a pink parasol from the basket at the back of the aisle, pop it open over Jesse's head, and process down the aisle beside him.

I briefly considered tackling Fern or running out and dragging him back by his ponytail, but I knew that would be more of a distraction. Even though I wanted to kill him, I knew it was best to play this off to the guests as if it was the plan all along. In his gold jacket, Fern looked every bit like a member of the wedding party.

"What does he think he's doing?" I asked, watching him weave his way down the aisle.

"Avoiding questioning." Reese's face was serious, and I knew this did not look good for Fern.

"Uh oh." Kate put her hands over her eyes as Fern stumbled, grabbing Jesse's arm to keep from falling. She ran off to the getting-ready room and returned a moment later, a shocked look on her face.

"What?" I asked, not sure I wanted to know.

"I may have crushed up some Valium in the last champagne bottle to help calm their nerves before the ceremony." Kate didn't meet my eyes. "I thought they might each have a last sip. I didn't know they'd drink the whole bottle before the ceremony."

I stared at Kate for a few moments before turning my attention to the bridal party standing at the front of the aisle. The groomsmaids looked glassy-eyed and swayed where they stood, and Jesse held one hand over his mouth as he giggled. Fern leaned against one of the pedestals holding a flower urn, the parasol in his other hand held high.

"Shalom," Rabbi Hoffman said, causing most of the audience to exchange glances and whispers. "We are gathered here today to celebrate one of life's greatest moments: the joining of two hearts."

Maybe this wouldn't be so bad, I told myself. Aside from the fact the hairdresser was standing next to the grooms, and the attendants looked like they might pass out, the ceremony might not be such a disaster after all.

"In this ceremony, we will witness the joining of . . ." Rabbi Hoffman paused and looked up at the two grooms in front of him and the women standing on either side of Stefan and Jesse. "Wait. Is this a double wedding?"

I closed my eyes as I heard Fern explain in a slurred stage whisper—and while hiccupping several times—Jesse was marrying Stefan.

The rabbi looked at the women again and put a hand up to his ear. "Which one is Jesse?"

More hiccups as Fern pointed to the brown-haired groom.

"It's unfortunate your rabbi is hard of hearing," Reese said.

"But a good thing Fern brought an umbrella." Kate pointed to the raindrops beginning to fall as guests opened their parasols. One of the groomsmaids had her head back and mouth open, and it looked like she was trying to catch the rain.

"Seriously with the Valium?" I asked Kate.

"One tiny pill." Kate held two fingers close together. "At least Stefan looks relaxed. Normally he'd be pitching a fit if he was getting rained on and being married by a rabbi who's trying to pair him off with one of his groomsmaids."

I looked to Fern, who no longer leaned against the floral pedestal. He had his arm outstretched so the pink parasol covered both grooms as they faced each other. Kate was right. Stefan's usual sneer was gone, replaced by a vacant smile. Maybe doping the bridal party hadn't been such a horrible idea after all, although I had no intention of admitting that to Kate.

"Is there anyone present who has just cause why this couple should not be united?" the rabbi asked.

Fern hiccupped loudly as he leaned against the flower pedestal again. He shook his head when the rabbi glanced over at him, and he pantomimed zipping up his lips. "Not me. Carry on, good sir."

I watched in growing horror as Fern's feet slowly slid lower. The parasol he held over the grooms' heads dropped so low they were squatting underneath it and looked half their normal height.

Kate tapped a finger on her chin. "Do you think the photographer can make them taller in all the photos?"

I felt my eyelid vibrate as I turned to Reese. "You might be dealing with more than one murder today, although, under the circumstances, I feel confident no jury in the world would find me guilty."

Reese looked at the grooms hunched underneath a pink parasol and the groomsmaid weaving her head as she tried to catch rain in her mouth. "I'd acquit you."

CHAPTER 6

I held my shoes in one hand as I tiptoed up the stairs to my fourth-floor apartment, my boxy metal emergency kit hanging from my shoulder, and the weight of it digging into my flesh. I wasn't sure which ached more—my feet after a long wedding day, or my shoulder after carrying my emergency kit in from my car. I sighed as I set the case down outside my apartment door and rubbed the grooves left in my shoulder.

The building was quiet, and the only hint there were other residents was the faint scent of pizza lingering in the air. I tried to keep my keys from jingling as I opened my door, sliding the case across the floor and inside with one foot instead of picking it up again.

The corner stone-front apartment building in Georgetown consisted of four floors with only two units per floor, mostly occupied by young professionals like me with a couple of retired longtime residents rounding out the group. I didn't know most of my neighbors other than to say hello or sign for a package if they were out. Except for one.

"There you are!" Leatrice's voice made me jump.

I tried not to groan out loud as I turned around to see my

octogenarian neighbor's platinum-blond head popping up from the stairwell. "You're still awake? It's almost one in the morning."

"*Matlock* marathon," she said. "And you know I always like to stay up on your wedding days and make sure you get home safely."

Ever since I'd moved into the building seven years ago, my first-floor neighbor had taken it upon herself to act as my substitute mother, matchmaker, and personal security detail. Leatrice was the unofficial den mother of the building and ran her own version of a neighborhood watch, which usually consisted of stalking people she deemed suspicious until they moved out.

"You don't have to do that," I said, purposely standing in the doorway of my apartment so she couldn't follow me inside. The last thing I needed after an arduous wedding was Leatrice drilling me about all the details.

She walked the last few steps to join me on my apartment's landing, and I did a double take. Unless I was a lot more tired than I thought and had started hallucinating, the tiny woman who barely reached my shoulder wore brown-footed pajamas with a tail. Even though she didn't have the floppy-eared hood pulled up on her head, I could tell they were dog pajamas. Chances were good she bought them in the kids' department.

"It's no trouble at all. Especially after what happened at your wedding." She rocked back and forth on her pajamaed feet.

"What do you mean?" I reached a hand inside my apartment and flipped on the lights, blinking a few times as the overhead light in my living room illuminated the yellow twill couch and matching oversized chair. I cringed as I noticed the piles of papers I'd left on the wooden dining room table earlier when I was going through the wedding files. I'd even left my empty Mocha Frappuccino bottle on the glass coffee table when I'd rushed out.

"The homicide of course."

How could I have forgotten Leatrice's police scanner? "You heard that?" I dropped my keys on the bookcase next to my front door and shoved my emergency case to the side as I stepped inside.

"A dead body called in from Meridian House?" She squeezed around me and hopped onto the couch, tucking her legs underneath her. "How could I miss it?"

I couldn't help flinching a little when she mentioned the dead body. The image of Cher Noble, her purple-shadowed eyes wide and unblinking, would not be one I'd purge from my brain anytime soon.

"Was Detective Reese there?" Leatrice asked, waggling her drawn-on eyebrows.

I deposited my black Longchamp bag on the floor next to the couch and headed to the kitchen. In the chaos of the wedding day, I'd barely eaten a thing. It hadn't bothered me at the time, but now I could feel my empty stomach rumbling.

I opened the refrigerator door and peered inside. "He was on duty."

"Well, wasn't that lucky? It's so nice when young couples get to work together these days."

I scanned my nearly empty shelves, grabbed a day-old Chinese takeout box, and closed the door. "We don't exactly work together." I didn't mention calling us an official couple might be premature.

"But since so many crimes seem to take place at your weddings, you get to see the detective a lot. Not everyone is so lucky."

Only Leatrice would see criminal activity at my weddings as a good thing. I lay the blame squarely on the shoulders of true crime TV. And *Matlock*.

"Do you want anything?" I called through the open space dividing my kitchen and living room as I dumped the container of lo mein on a plate and popped it into the microwave. "I have leftover Chinese."

"No thank you, dearie, but you go right ahead."

I grabbed a wine goblet I'd rinsed and set upside down to dry on the counter earlier in the week and filled it from an opened bottle of pinot noir. I stepped out of my black flats, leaving them in the kitchen once the microwave dinged, and I retrieved my plate and headed for the living room. "I didn't get a chance to eat all day, even though Richard had special meals for all the vendors."

"Richard was there?" Leatrice asked. "How did he handle seeing your boyfriend? I know it's been hard for him after things didn't work out between you two in the romance department."

Leatrice had never been able to understand Richard and I were best friends, and there was never any potential for us in the romance department. In her mind, if a man and woman were attractive, young, and single, there was always potential. I'd never had the heart to explain to Leatrice that Richard and I were both looking for Mr. Right.

"He's getting used to the idea." I sat down on the couch next to Leatrice and put my wine glass on the coffee table. I began pulling the bobby pins out of my bun until my hair fell loose around my shoulders. It felt great to let it down after having it pulled up all day. "You know he's seeing someone too."

"I'm so glad you're both moving on." Leatrice patted my knee. "Now tell me about the murder."

I swirled the lo mein noodles onto my fork and blew on them. "I don't know how much I should be telling you. It's still an open investigation."

Leatrice produced a small spiral notebook from her pajama pocket and flipped it open. "The police got the call around five o'clock."

I took a bite of noodles and washed it down with a too-large gulp of wine, which made me cough. "You took notes?"

"The basics. I still don't know who was killed."

"I guess it's pretty common knowledge by now it was our officiant who was strangled."

Leatrice gasped. "Someone murdered a man of the cloth?"

"Technically our man of the cloth was a man dressed as a woman. Actually, a three-hundred-pound drag queen dressed like Cher."

Leatrice's brightly colored mouth fell open. "I know I haven't been to church in a while, but they've sure changed it since my day."

"Cher Noble wasn't affiliated with a church. She got ordained over the internet to perform weddings in drag."

Leatrice bobbed her head as she absorbed this. "And someone killed her at the wedding? Before or after the ceremony?"

"Before." I took another bite of the savory noodles.

"So did you have to call off the wedding?" Leatrice asked.

I shook my head. "We called in a backup officiant and moved the entire event to the historic house next door."

"Well aren't you clever?" Leatrice grinned at me. "So no one was the wiser?"

"I wouldn't say that." I took a sip of wine. "Our new officiant was a Jewish rabbi who didn't know it was a gay wedding until the last minute and tried to marry the grooms off to their female attendants. We may have actually held a double wedding. I still can't be sure."

Leatrice giggled. "You really do have the most exciting job, dear."

"I wish it was a little less exciting sometimes," I admitted. "At this point a desk job in a cubicle doesn't sound so bad."

Leatrice tapped her notebook on her leg. "So tell me more about the murder. Do the police think it was a crime of opportunity or passion?"

I set my plate down on the coffee table. I definitely was not going to say Fern knew the victim since I didn't put it past her to show up on his doorstep with a list of questions. "I really shouldn't be talking about the case. Anyway, I don't know much more than you."

A rap on the door made me jump.

"Who would be visiting you at this time of night?" Leatrice asked, getting up and padding over to the door.

I didn't point out Leatrice was also visiting me in the middle of the night.

She opened the door a crack before pulling it open all the way. Detective Reese stood in the doorway in the same clothes he'd had on earlier, the gray shirt a bit more rumpled and his dark wavy hair more tousled. He gave me a weary smile over Leatrice's head.

I felt my pulse quicken.

"We were talking about your latest case, Detective," Leatrice said, waving him into my apartment with a flourish of her arm.

To his credit, Reese didn't look surprised by Leatrice's pajamas or by the fact she knew about the murder. Like me, Reese had learned not to be shocked by anything Leatrice did.

"Did you finish with the paperwork?" I asked when I'd found my voice.

He nodded and stepped inside. "I thought I'd stop by on my way home and make sure you were okay."

I knew my apartment was nowhere close to the route he took to go home from the police station. I tried not to smile too widely. "Do you want a glass of wine?"

He let out a breath. "I would love one."

I took my plate to the kitchen while he sat down on the couch. I pulled a second wine goblet down from my cabinets, checked it for dust, and filled it with pinot noir. When I returned to the living room, Leatrice was in full interrogation mode.

"Is this the first time you've seen a feather boa used as a murder weapon?" she asked.

I handed Reese his glass and squeezed myself in on the couch between him and Leatrice. He draped one arm around my shoulders and I leaned into him, letting myself relax for the first time all day.

He took a sip of wine. "You know I can't discuss an active investigation."

Leatrice's face fell.

"But I can confirm Annabelle's crime scenes are always the most interesting ones."

I twisted around and gave him a look. "Hey! Do you actually talk about 'Annabelle's crime scenes' down at the station?"

He shook his head and laughed. "No. You know I try to keep your name out of it."

I did know he tried to keep the fact he was dating a former witness/person of interest/suspect on the down low. I met his eyes and saw they'd deepened from hazel to green, and I couldn't help dropping my own eyes to his lips.

"Would you look at the time?" Leatrice stood up. "*Perry Mason* starts in a few minutes."

I turned and felt myself blush as I watched Leatrice open the door. "See you later, Leatrice."

She winked at me as she pulled the door closed behind her, and I knew Reese had seen it.

He leaned forward as he set his wine glass on the coffee table. "It's not that I don't like hanging out with your neighbor . . ." His words trailed off as he nuzzled my neck.

I did my best not to moan out loud. "I'm glad you showed up when you did. Otherwise she might have tried to have a sleepover."

He laughed as he kissed behind my ear. "That would have been awkward."

I turned around to face him, and he pulled me so I was sitting on his lap.

He ran his hands up through my hair. "Especially since I was hoping to have a sleepover."

My heart hammered in my chest as he kissed me deeply, and I let him lower me back onto the couch.

CHAPTER 7

"Rise and shine!" Kate's voice pulled me from my sleep, and I pushed myself up, blinking and rubbing my eyes as I looked around my living room. The soft angora throw covering me slipped from my shoulders, and I tried to tug it back up with one hand. From the bright sunlight streaming in my windows and the sounds of traffic from the street below, I could tell it was sometime in the midmorning.

It took me a few seconds to realize my dress was lying on the floor, and I was lifting myself up off Reese's bare chest. He mumbled something unintelligible and tried to pull me back down.

"We've got company," I whispered to him as Kate fumbled with her key and shoved my front door open.

When I'd given Kate a key to my place, it had been so she could have access to the office to drop things off or pick things up when I was busy. I'd never imagined this scenario. From the look on her face when she spotted me with Reese on the couch, neither had she. She stood unmoving in the doorway in a short Lily Pulitzer sundress, high-heel pink mules, and sunglasses resting on the top of her head. She held keys in one hand and a to-go coffee holder in the other.

"Annabelle!" Her expression of surprise turned to one of delight. "I guess it's safe to say you're not ready for brunch."

I wrapped the pale-green throw around me so only my bra straps showed and sat up all the way, leaving Reese lying on my couch in nothing but his black pants.

He rubbed his eyes. "Is there anyone who doesn't have a key to your apartment? Aside from me?"

Kate shut the door behind her. "You haven't given him a key yet? Even Leatrice has one."

I shot her a look as I ran a hand through my hair. "She's my neighbor and she made one herself using her home spy kit."

Reese laughed as he sat up. "It's okay. I don't mind knocking, although apparently no one else knows how."

Kate ogled his well-muscled chest until I cleared my throat pointedly at her. *Sorry*, she mouthed with a shrug.

"I didn't expect Annabelle to have company or to forget we're meeting Richard and Fern for brunch." She held out the corrugated beverage holder to him and indicated one of the tall paper cups with a lid. "Here. You can have my mocha. You need it more than I do."

Reese shook his head as he looked around on the floor for his shirt. "I'm fine, but thanks."

Kate tapped her foot on the floor. "Take it. Consider it a thank you from me."

Reese narrowed his eyes at her as he wiggled the cup out of the holder. "A thank you for what?"

Kate's eyes wandered back to Reese's bare chest and arms, and she sighed. "Just thank you."

Oh, for the love of God. I rolled my eyes at her and hunted around at my feet until I found his wrinkled gray shirt. "You'd better put this on before you have to file a harassment complaint against my assistant."

Reese blushed as he slipped on his shirt and began buttoning it.

Kate held the remaining to-go coffee out to me and I took it gratefully, letting the heat warm my fingers. "What time is it anyway?"

"We still have a few minutes. I forgot how little traffic there is on Sunday morning. Plus, I found parking right in front of your building. That never happens in Georgetown. Part of me doesn't ever want to move my car because I'll never get such a good space again."

I took a sip of my mocha and closed my eyes as I swallowed the sweet coffee. "We can take my car if you want. I had to park six blocks away last night."

Reese frowned as he stood up. "You walked that far by yourself at one o'clock in the morning?"

"You know Saturday night in Georgetown," I said. "I did have my emergency kit, though." I pointed to the heavy metal case still sitting by the door. "One swing and I could take someone out."

Reese shook his head. "Next time you need to come home late, you call me and I'll walk you, okay?" He met my eyes and brushed a strand of hair off my face, and I felt my mouth go dry.

He jerked a thumb toward my hallway. "Do you mind if I pop into the bathroom before I head out?"

I shook my head as I found my voice. "It's all yours."

Kate watched him walk down the hall and disappear into the bathroom. "I love how he's so protective and a little forceful." She pointed to her bare arms. "Look. Goosebumps."

I ignored her as I stood up, wrapping the throw tighter around me. "If you breathe a word about this to Richard, I'll kill you."

Kate flopped onto the overstuffed chair across from the couch. "You don't need to worry about me. I have no desire to witness a Richard meltdown."

I walked into my kitchen carrying the two empty wine glasses from the night before with the angora throw trailing behind me. "He wouldn't melt down, would he?"

"No, you're right. If he walked in on you partially undressed and lying on top of a hot cop, he might drop dead."

I thought about disagreeing with Kate but realized she might be right. Richard was not known for his under reactions. I put the wine goblets in the sink and returned to the living room, scooping up my black dress from the floor and stepping into it without dropping the throw.

"You're wearing yesterday's dress to brunch?" Kate asked, crossing her legs so her dress rode up even further.

I pulled the dress over my hips and slipped my arms through. "No, but this is slightly less revealing than an open-weave throw. I'll hop in the shower and change once Reese is done in the bathroom."

Kate put a hand to her heart. "Whew. I was worried I was going to have to give you the fashion talk again."

"You mean the one where you tell me I don't show enough leg or cleavage?" I zipped up the side of the dress and draped the angora blanket over the back of the couch.

Kate snapped her fingers. "That's the one, but I was going to add a part about wearing too much black and recycling your look."

Before I could sit back down, there was a knock on the door. I opened the door, fully expecting to see Leatrice. I was wrong.

"I couldn't wait until the restaurant to talk to you." Fern rushed into the room, wringing his hands, with Richard behind him. "I'm a wreck."

For a wreck, he looked quite put together. He wore a sapphire-blue blazer with a yellow-and-blue-striped ascot, a yellow vest, and buff-colored pants. Richard looked equally as stylish in a beige linen suit with pant creases so sharp they looked like they could draw blood. He carried his bulging leather man bag by the handle instead of across his chest.

"What happened?" I asked.

Fern spun around. "What happened? You mean aside from Cher being murdered?"

"Why don't you sit down?" Kate said, standing up to give him her chair.

"Sit down? Sit down?" His voice rose a few octaves. "I can't sit down at a time like this."

"Richard?" I jerked my head toward the couch.

"I can't sit down, either." He set his black bag on the couch and waved his hands over his suit. "This suit wrinkles if you breathe on it wrong." He went over to the wall and leaned against it, keeping his legs completely straight so he looked like a human ramp.

"I thought you told me linen wrinkles were money wrinkles," I said.

"Normally, yes, but this linen is woven from a special flax plant, and I do not want it creased the first time I wear it."

"I get it," Kate said. "It's like how careful you are with a new car until you get your first ding."

Richard inhaled sharply. "I hope you aren't comparing my designer jacket to your Honda."

His bag rolled onto its side and the flap opened, revealing Richard's tiny Yorkie, Hermes. Hermes gave a little yip in greeting and ran back and forth on the couch, obviously excited to be out of the bag. I reached down and rubbed his head, and he gave my hand a quick lick.

Kate took one of Fern's hands in her own as he paced in a small circle. "We're all upset about Cher, but the police are working hard to find out who killed her."

"Are they?" He pulled a handkerchief matching his ascot from his inside jacket pocket and dabbed at his eyes.

"Of course they are." Kate led him to the chair. "But you know it's the early stages of the investigation. I'm sure we'll all be interviewed again."

"Again?" Fern tucked the handkerchief back into his jacket. "Some of us weren't interviewed a first time."

"Some of us were passed out drunk during the interviews," Richard said under his breath.

"What if they don't find who did it? You know how over-worked the DC police department is." Fern fluttered his hands in the air as he began pacing again. Hermes scampered from one end of the couch to the other, turning at the exact time Fern did each time. "How often have we had to help them solve cases?"

I wasn't sure if we'd always helped the police or made things harder, but we had been known to uncover clues the cops couldn't. Mostly because we were willing to skirt the law.

"Promise me, girls." Fern looked from Kate to me.

"Promise you what?" I asked.

Fern pressed his fingers to his ascot. "We'll find out who killed Cher even if the police give up."

"It hasn't even been twenty-four hours." I lowered my voice. "And you know I'm not supposed to get mixed up in police inves-tigations anymore."

Richard crossed his arms and his ruffled shirt cuffs poked out of the sleeves of his jacket. "When has that ever stopped you?" he drawled, unfolding his arms and quickly smoothing out the linen fabric of his jacket where wrinkles had already started to form.

"He has a point," Kate said.

I tried to signal Kate with a pointed eye roll in the direction of the bathroom and hoped Reese wasn't able to hear any of this. "You know I promised Detective Reese."

"What did you do just now?" Fern narrowed his eyes at me then did a double take. "Annabelle, sweetie, are you wearing the same dress you wore yesterday?"

I let out a breath, relieved my fashion 'don't' had distracted him. "I'm not wearing this to brunch. I slipped it on when Kate arrived. I was about to hop in the shower and change when you arrived."

Richard pushed himself away from the wall and took a few steps toward me, picking a bit of beige carpet lint off my shoulder. "Did you sleep in your clothes?"

Hermes put his front paws on the arm of the sofa, stretching his little black-and-brown head so he could sniff at me. After snuffling at my sleeve for a moment, he yipped.

"Hermes agrees with me," Richard said. "Something's up."

"Traitor," I mumbled at the dog who grinned at me with his pink tongue hanging out of his mouth.

Kate raised her hand. "I can personally attest to the fact she did *not* sleep in her clothes."

Fern studied my face and touched a hand to my hair. "Traces of makeup. Tousled hair. Flushed cheeks." He tapped a finger to his chin. "If I didn't know better I'd think you . . ." He shrieked and slapped a hand over his mouth, his eyes darting around the room.

"Busted," Kate said in a singsong voice.

Fern dropped his hands from his mouth, his eyes wide. "Is Detective Hottie here or did he already leave?"

"Is the detective here right now?" Richard asked, his eyes scanning the room as if he expected Reese to pop out from behind the furniture.

I didn't answer. It was bad enough Kate knew. Fern's questioning would be unbearable, and Richard's look of shock was already making me squirm.

"What's the big deal?" Kate asked Fern. "I thought you liked Reese. You're always saying you wouldn't mind if he frisked you."

Fern snapped his fingers at Kate. "I wasn't a witness in a murder case."

"It's not like you saw anything," I said. "The police only want to talk to you because you were at the wedding and you knew Cher."

"That's just it, Annabelle." Fern nibbled on the corner of his lower lip. "I did see something."

"What?" Kate, Richard, and I said in unison.

"Well, I didn't *see* something but I know something. The last time I saw Cher, she told me she was being stalked."

Kate's mouth dropped open. "Did she say who was stalking her?"

Fern shook his head. "She didn't know, but she'd gotten threatening messages."

I touched Fern's arm. "You have to tell the police."

"I know, I know. I was going to go down to the station today, but Richard convinced me not to."

"I merely said it wouldn't hurt to wait until after brunch." Richard said with a sniff. "It isn't like the police will have done much since last night. And it's Sunday morning. They probably haven't even made their first doughnut run."

"But what if I get in trouble for withholding evidence?" Fern bit his thumbnail. "I should have said something yesterday."

"You're right." Detective Reese's deep voice made us all jump. He stood where the hall met the kitchen with his arms folded across his chest and his expression serious. "You should have said something."

Fern shrieked and took off for the door, knocking into Richard, who stumbled before looking down at his suit and crying, "Wrinkles!" as he fell to the floor with a thud. He'd twisted quickly enough to land on the side of one arm, but had rolled just as quickly onto his stomach. He now lay face-down with his arms stiff by his side as he moaned. Hermes leapt off the couch and ran over, alternately licking Richard's face and yipping.

Kate stared down at Richard's motionless body and cringed. "That had to hurt."

I heard Fern's footsteps as he barreled down the stairs of my building, still shrieking. I looked over at Reese, who was doing a bad job of containing a smirk. "You sure know how to make an entrance."

CHAPTER 8

"Tell me everything you know about Cher Noble's stalker," I said as we waited to be seated at Blue Duck Tavern, the sleek and stylish restaurant inside the sleek and stylish Park Hyatt hotel in upper Georgetown. Midday light from the two walls of tall uncovered windows filled the restaurant, which held a mix of long rectangular walnut tables and smaller rounds surrounded by Shaker-style chairs and benches.

"Didn't you hear what I said to the detective?" Fern asked.

"You mean when Leatrice dragged you back upstairs?" Kate asked.

My first-floor neighbor had been so startled by Fern's shrieking, she'd rushed from her apartment and made a citizen's arrest, escorting him back to my apartment in plastic handcuffs. No doubt it had been the highlight of her year.

Fern drew one finger across his eyebrow. "I've decided to forgive the old dear. I know she's been unduly influenced by true crime TV."

"Well, I missed everything you told Reese," I said. "I was busy making Richard an ice pack and finding him the right shade of concealer."

Richard touched a hand to his nose, which was still puffy from its impact with my floor. "I can't believe I'm wearing drugstore makeup. Talk about insult to injury."

I ignored Richard's slight and inhaled deeply, breathing in the scent of sugar coming from the open-air pastry kitchen where I knew they were turning out pecan sticky buns and homemade doughnuts glazed with bourbon maple syrup. My stomach growled in anticipation.

Kate patted Richard's arm. "You can hardly notice your nose, by the way."

"Really?" he asked, his eyes scanning the bustling restaurant buzzing with chatter from a mix of DC establishment and boozy brunch ladies.

I knew he was checking to see if any of the other guests were clients. An encounter with a DC society matron would be the last thing Richard would want on a day he was looking less than perfect. He shifted his man bag from one hand to the other, but it no longer bulged at the sides from the weight of Hermes. We'd left the pup with Leatrice, since she adored him, and we'd found not all restaurants welcomed dogs at brunch.

"Of course. Annabelle's expired makeup did the trick," Kate said. "Anyway, it's good for all of us to get out and get our minds off things."

"Anything is better than being dragged down to the police station." Fern shuddered. "I suppose I owe your boyfriend one for not taking me in for questioning today."

"You were lucky he wasn't going in to work today," I said, knowing the last thing Reese wanted to do after working a murder scene all day on Saturday was to deal with a hysterical hairdresser on his day off.

"Too bad he couldn't join us," Kate said.

Richard made a face. I knew he wasn't sad Reese had opted out of brunch, but I hoped if I ignored his attitude he'd warm up to me seeing someone. This strategy had never worked before, mind you. When it came to juggling Richard and other men, I usually kept a Chinese firewall between the two.

"He has plans to watch some sort of sports with his brother," I said. I also knew brunch with my crew was not Reese's idea of a relaxing Sunday. Richard was so jealous he could barely look at him, and Kate couldn't seem to stop herself from looking at him.

Kate's eyes lit up. "How is his hunky big brother?"

We'd all met Reese's older but equally handsome brother, Daniel Reese, when he'd done security for a past wedding. He'd also accompanied Mike to join us in Bali a couple of months ago, and Kate had planted a juicy one on him. It had been a spur-of-the-moment kiss and hadn't led anywhere. A part of me was glad since I could imagine the potential awkwardness of the two of us dating brothers.

"He's good, I guess," I said. "I really haven't seen him since Bali."

"Too busy?" Kate nudged me.

Fern swiveled to face me. "I never did ask you, Annabelle. Why was the detective at your place this morning if he wasn't planning on joining us?"

I opened and closed my mouth. "Looks like they have a table for us," I said finally as a hostess in a snug black dress waved for us to follow her.

I let out a sigh of relief as we were led past the open pastry kitchen where individual apple pies sat cooling on the white-and-gray-marble island while chefs in white caps peeled bright-green Granny Smiths. We descended a couple of steps and were shown to a table for four against a window overlooking the restaurant patio. Even though the weather was still a touch too cool for my liking, and I wore a pink cardigan over my sleeveless green sheath dress, the cream-colored market umbrellas shading the outside tables were open, and a few guests sat underneath them.

"So tell me again why you didn't break your fall with your hands," I said to Richard as he took the chair next to mine and draped his jacket over the back of his chair.

"I'll have you know not only is this suit couture, it's Irish linen. If I'd bent my arms suddenly the fabric would have creased. Possibly permanently." He patted my hand. "You wouldn't understand since all your clothes are wash-and-wear, darling."

Fern appraised the suit from across the table. "Is it Canali?"

"Ermenegildo Zegna," Richard said with a sniff.

"Are they speaking in code?" Kate whispered to me.

"You made the right call," Fern said, adjusting the French cuffs of his shirt. "The jacket is perfection."

"Thank you." Richard dropped one of his hands to his lap and kept the other cupped around his nose. "I wouldn't have fallen if Fern hadn't been startled by Detective Reese."

Fern fanned himself with his napkin. "For a moment I thought he was going to cuff me and drag me away."

"That doesn't sound so bad," Kate muttered from behind her menu.

A waiter in a black suit approached us and placed a ceramic bowl filled with sliced French bread in the middle of the table alongside a small square plate of butter. "Can I start you off with beverages? We're featuring mango or strawberry sorbet mimosas and Bloody Marys for brunch, as well as Bloody Marias."

"Bloody Marias?" Kate asked.

"A Bloody Mary with tequila," the waiter explained.

"I should not do tequila." Kate made a face. "It makes my inhibitions fly out the window."

"I didn't know you had any inhibitions left," Richard said, giving her a sticky smile. "A sorbet mimosa for me, please."

"Why don't we do four sorbet mimosas?" I said before Kate could zing one back to Richard. "Two mango and two strawberry."

I reached for a slice of bread after the waiter left and was pleased to find it still warm. I spread the soft butter across the surface and took a bite, savoring the yeasty crunch.

"Back to Reese." Richard leaned back in his chair. "Why would he have arrested you?"

"He was not going to arrest Fern," I said. "He only wants to question him about Cher Noble's stalker."

The waiter returned with our mimosas and set the filled goblets on the table. Scoops of red and yellow sorbet bobbed in the bubbly, and rock candy stirrers were submerged inside the cocktails. Kate picked the mango version and swirled the sugar stirrer around in her glass before taking a sip and smiling.

Fern picked a strawberry mimosa. "You know I've known Cher for years."

Richard waved a hand to indicate I should take my pick of the final two mimosas. I selected the mango and swiveled the rock candy around the bottom. "How exactly did you get to know her?"

"I styled her wigs. Lots of the girls drop their hair off for me to work on after hours."

It made sense. I'd never seen a drag queen set foot in Fern's upscale Georgetown hair salon, nor had I seen him styling headless wigs. I remembered the day I'd discovered Fern was often called by funeral homes to style hair for his dead clients, and I realized there was more to his job than met the eye. This was more evidence to the fact.

"So you're in with the drag queen crowd?" Kate asked.

"You could say that," Fern said. "They're a welcome break from the social climbing tramps I have to deal with in the salon."

It no longer startled me when Fern referred to his clients—and members of my bridal parties—as tramps, hussies, or tarts. Even though I knew I'd get fired in a hot minute if I said the same thing, the women seemed to consider it part of Fern's refreshing charm.

"So when did Cher mention she had a stalker?" I asked.

Fern drummed his fingers along his jaw. "It must have been

two weeks ago. She was picking up her wigs, and I noticed her acting jumpy."

Kate leaned forward. "Jumpy how?"

"It was in the salon after I'd closed, but she kept looking over her shoulder at the door like she expected someone to walk in," Fern said. "I asked her what was wrong, and she said she thought she was being followed."

"How odd," I said. "Why would someone be following her?"

"She wouldn't say, but she told me one of her tires had been slashed a few days earlier." Fern drained half of his mimosa. "Although, to be fair, she lives in a dodgy neighborhood."

"Could it have been a hate crime?" I asked.

"Possibly, but she didn't go around dressed as Cher unless she was performing, so I don't know if anyone in her neighborhood would know about her alter ego." Fern took another long drink and set his empty glass on the table. "In her regular life, she was a he who worked at the Department of Treasury."

"I did not see that coming." Kate took the last sip of her drink and put the glass next to Fern's.

"So her death could be unconnected to the drag queen part of her life?" Richard asked.

"Maybe she was a spy and the Cher act was her cover," Kate said, her voice lowered.

Fern shook his head as he waved down our waiter and signaled for another round of drinks. "I don't think she was a spy. She'd been a drag queen long before she got a job with the government."

Kate frowned. "Too bad. It would have been fun to be caught up in a spy caper."

"Speak for yourself," I said. "I promised Reese I wouldn't get caught up in any kind of investigation. I'm pretty sure undercover spy capers count."

Fern looked at me. "You weren't serious, were you?"

"Of course I was." I licked my rock sugar stirrer to get the last few drops of mimosa as a waiter put a full replacement down in front of me. "Reese will kill me if he catches me poking around in his case."

Kate raised her second mimosa in a silent toast. "Only if he catches you."

"Which he always does," I reminded her. "We aren't great at staying undercover ourselves."

Fern hiccupped. "But we owe it to Cher to find out who killed her. I can't bear the thought of someone strangling her and getting away with it."

I put my hand on top of his. "They won't. I promise you the police will find the killer."

Fern swiped at his eyes. "And if they don't, we will?"

Kate put her hand on top of both of ours. "You know you can count on us."

"I am not part of this," Richard said, shaking his head. "Meddling in a police investigation is a crime, and I do not hear good things about the cuisine at the DC jails."

"Are you all in trouble again?"

I recognized the Southern drawl and turned to see a pair of tall blondes walk up to our table, both with stick-straight hair and Louis Vuitton totes hooked on their arms.

Fern blinked hard and glanced at his two empty mimosa glasses. "These drinks are stronger than I thought. Is anyone else seeing double?"

"Botox Barbie," Kate muttered. "And she brought a clone."

The owner of Brides by Brianna flinched, and I knew she'd heard Kate. I forced myself to smile. "Hi, Brianna. What can we do for you?"

Brianna had burst onto the wedding planner scene the year before and had been nothing but a thorn in our sides ever since. If she wasn't trying to steal our brides, she was spreading gossip about us.

"Nothing." She waved a hand in the direction of the other

woman. "I thought I'd introduce Tina Pink, owner of TP Inc. We're here having brunch with our husbands." She waved her hand at two dark-haired men at a table behind us who both looked like they could have stepped off the set of *The Sopranos*. "Like you."

I could see Kate bristle at the implication Fern and Richard were our husbands, and I reached underneath the table and put a hand on her knee.

"What an unfortunate name for a company," Richard said without looking up.

The second blonde flipped her hair off her shoulder as two splotches of red appeared on her cheeks. "My company is pronounced T Pink like my name, by the way."

"What happened to you?" Brianna asked, gaping at Richard.

His hands flew to his nose. "The girls promised me it wasn't noticeable."

Briana laughed. "Well, they lied. You look like you could lead Santa's sleigh."

Fern gave Brianna a fake smile. "I thought maybe this was one of your new girls." Fern used air quotations when he said the word "girls."

Brianna glanced around her. "How many times do I have to tell you? Those call girl rumors were completely made up."

Fern raised his shoulders and both hands as if he didn't believe her, but I knew he did since he'd been the one to help spread the rumors Kate had made up.

"If I were you, I'd be worried about my own company's reputation." Brianna leaned close to me. "Especially since you can't do a wedding without someone getting murdered."

The two women flounced back to their table without a glance behind them. I glared at their retreating backs, hating them for being right. Dead bodies were not good for business.

CHAPTER 9

"How is it possible to hate someone so much after only meeting them once?" Kate asked as she wound her way through Georgetown traffic the next morning, honking her car horn if the drivers in front of her attempted to make a left turn.

I clutched the car door as we swerved around a double-parked delivery truck. "Tina Pink being besties with Brianna doesn't help. Guilt by association."

Kate made a face as she gunned it through a yellow traffic light while it turned red, and a cacophony of horns sounded behind us. "Brianna or no Brianna, I didn't like the look of her. And how have we never heard of her before?"

I took a tentative sip of my to-go mocha as we drove past the Washington Harbor and underneath the Whitehurst Freeway, skirting the Potomac River on our right, the dark water glistening in the sun. I spotted a pair of kayakers cutting through the water and took another sip of coffee, glad for the warmth and the sweetness. Even though the weather was warming, I knew the Potomac was still freezing and felt glad to be inside a car with hot coffee and not out on the water.

"I'll bet Richard will know more about her today," I said.

We were on our way to the offices of Richard Gerard Catering for a tasting with Darla and Debbie, a mother-daughter duo we'd worked with the year before. Debbie's wedding to Turner Grant the Third had been as over-the-top and alcohol infused as the bride and her mother, but the WASPy duo remained one of our favorite clients, because they had deep pockets and appreciated everything we did for them.

Not even a year after Debbie became Mrs. Turner Grant the Third, Darla called us to plan the baby shower for the expectant mother. Wedding Belles did not normally plan baby showers or first birthday parties or mitzvahs or anything involving children, but we always made exceptions for cherished clients. Especially ones who had a sense of fun and money to burn.

"You're right." Kate reached for her coffee in the center console's cup holder. "Richard's had almost twenty-four hours to get all the information on her. If there's dirt out there, he'll have it."

I put a hand over my eyes to shield them from the bright sun as we veered around the Lincoln Memorial and onto Independence Avenue. "Funny how quickly Brianna latched onto her. There must be something in it for her."

"You're right. Botox Barbie does not do things out of the goodness of her heart." Kate took off the sunglasses perched on the top of her head and handed them to me. This still left the oversized tortoiseshell pair on her face. "You want to use these?"

"Do you mind me asking why you have on two pairs of sunglasses?"

She shrugged. "They make a great headband, but they're much cooler than actual headbands. I mean, it isn't the 90s anymore. Don't worry. I wasn't going to wear two pairs into the tasting. Richard would never let me live it down."

She was right. Richard was our own personal fashion police, and

I often got verbal citations from him. I was grateful he'd stopped handing out the written ones. I took Kate's headband sunglasses, slipped them on, and let my eyes adjust to the darker view.

My phone trilled and I dug it out of my bag, groaning when I recognized the number. "Cara Cox," I told Kate. "Wonder what she wants?"

"I don't know," we both said in unison and laughed.

'I don't know' was this mother of the bride's answer to any question. It had taken months for her to sign a single contract because she couldn't make a decision, and we'd had so many walk-throughs at their venue the manager threatened to charge us the next time she tried to pop by.

"Hi, Cara," I said. "How are you?"

"I don't know, Annabelle. I really don't."

I pressed a hand over the phone's mouthpiece so she wouldn't hear Kate's giggling.

"Do you think we should revisit the catering proposal?" Cara asked.

"I don't think we need to revisit it, but I do know you need to sign off on the final menu. The wedding is in three weeks."

Cara sighed. "I don't know."

"I know the wedding can't go ahead without final contracts signed," I said, trying to keep my voice firm. "Do you want the wedding to be called off because you didn't have any vendors booked?"

"I don't know, I mean, no, of course not."

We passed the Capitol Building, and I glanced up at the white-marble-domed building—one of the tallest in the city but still only about half as tall the Washington Monument. Kate made a hard right a few blocks down and began hunting for street parking.

"I need to go into a meeting, Cara, but I will need those signed by close of business today."

"I don't know. Maybe we should do another walk-through . . ." Cara began, but I clicked off the phone.

"So is there a chance we'll have the weekend off in a few weeks?" Kate asked. "A full weekend would really help with my dating schedule."

"Probably not. Even if Mrs. I Don't Know can't get her act together, I have a feeling the bride and groom will."

Kate frowned. "Wishful drinking on my part."

"Something like that." I shook my head. "Are you saying working for me is cramping your social life?"

"Yes." Kate let out a breath. "Thanks for finally noticing."

I shook my head. "If this is what your cramped social life looks like, I'm afraid to see what it would be like otherwise."

Kate winked at me as she angled her car into a snug spot across from the Richard Gerard Catering offices. "Be very afraid."

She straightened out and lightly tapped the bumper in front of us before putting the car in park.

"Thanks for driving today." I looked at the other car's bumper and felt relieved there was no dent.

"No problem. I couldn't stay parked in front of your building forever."

Kate had let me switch out my car for hers before we left, so now I had the prime parking spot in front of my building. I smoothed out my blue-floral print fit-and-flare dress as I stepped out of the car, hanging my black Kate Spade purse in the crook of my arm.

Kate traded her flat driving shoes for a pair of three-inch peep-toe nude heels and adjusted the scoop neckline of her celadon-green tank dress. Even after the adjustment, I still saw plenty of cleavage.

Kate led the way across the street to the painted brick townhouse with the metal nameplate by the door reading "Richard Gerard Catering." She rapped her knuckles on the glass panes of the front door, rubbing her bare arms and stamping her feet to keep warm in the cool morning air.

Richard flung open the door and waved us inside. "Thank goodness you got here before the client. I can't decide which signature cocktail works better for a carousel theme."

For Debbie's carousel-themed baby shower, we were decorating Darla's house with actual vintage carousel horses, mirroring the walls, and serving gourmet versions of carnival food. The decor alone would cost more than most weddings.

I walked from the townhouse's foyer into the adjoining tasting room and blinked a few times to get my bearings. The walls, which were normally painted in a shade of brackish green Richard referred to as "Baby's First Summer," were draped in pink-and-white-striped fabric. The table where we would be sitting to taste the menu had a round striped tent over it topped with a pink pennant and a shiny gold carousel horse as a centerpiece. No one could say Richard wasn't embracing the carnival theme.

I peeked at his nose as subtly as I could. Almost no swelling and the redness was gone. I suspected he'd availed himself of high-end concealer, but if he did the look was flawless.

Richard led us to a mirrored bar and held out two cocktails. "So I've taken inspiration from the famous Carousel bar in New Orleans, of course."

"Of course," Kate said, picking up a martini glass filled with purple liquid and topped with white foam and a candied violet.

"You're tasting Eudora Welty's Purple Hat cocktail." He put a hand on Kate's arm. "The clients aren't allergic to eggs, are they?"

Kate paused with the drink halfway to her lips. "Is that relevant to this drink?"

"Where do you think the foam comes from?" Richard asked, tilting the glass up to her lips for her. "But you can't taste the egg white."

I picked up a peach-hued drink in a rocks glass with a few

small leaves floating on top. As I raised it to my mouth, I could smell the mint.

"And you're drinking my version of the Fleur de Lis, Annabelle." Richard put his hands on his hips as he watched us sip. "So, what do you think?"

"Delicious," I said, swallowing the cocktail and tasting hints of lemon and possibly ginger ale. "And not too sweet."

Richard smiled. "The original Fleur de Lis called for a cucumber wedge, but I know Debbie and Darla don't like food in their drinks."

"And the egg?" Kate asked, taking another sip of her drink.

Richard winked at her. "What they don't know can't hurt them, darling."

I leaned one elbow against the bar. "So, I know you haven't been worrying about these cocktails since yesterday. What do you know about Tina Pink?"

Richard pressed a hand to his heart. "Are you implying I dug up dirt on a new planner because she was unpleasant to us yesterday?"

I tilted my head and gave him a look. "Are you implying you didn't?"

Richard laughed. "You know me too well." He led us to a sleek gray couch—the only thing in the room untouched by the carousel decor. "For starters, she's not a new planner. Up until about three weeks ago, she worked for Melody Hunter."

"From Melody's Mitzvahs?" Kate asked, perching on one end of the couch and crossing her legs so her skirt slid up to midthigh.

"Tina had a noncompete," Richard continued. "But the word on the street is she started booking her own events before Melody had a clue she wanted to leave."

Kate made a tsk-ing sound. "People have no loyalty anymore."

"That's why she looked familiar," I said, leaning back on the couch. "Aside from being a Brianna clone, I must have seen her with Melody at industry events."

"And now she's switching over from mitzvahs to weddings?" Kate asked, finishing her drink and setting the empty martini glass on the wooden cocktail table.

"A little bit of everything. Corporate, mitzvahs, weddings." Richard wrinkled his nose. "From what I hear, she's desperate for anything and will slit your throat to get your clients."

Kate put a hand to her neck. "How gruesome."

Jim, Richard's top catering captain, came into the room with a tray of hors d'oeuvres. He dropped the white, flat board to our level and I could see it held miniature cones. "Spicy tuna in a sesame cone?"

"Thank you." I took a cone and admired the crimson tuna mixture mounded perfectly inside. I tuned my attention back to Richard. "Don't mention throats around Fern. You know he's still sensitive about Cher Noble being strangled."

Jim jerked as if he'd been slapped, and the tray of cones nearly spilled into Kate's lap. "I'm so sorry," he stammered. "I must have had a muscle spasm."

Richard shot him a dirty look but recovered with a smile. "No harm done. Why don't you leave the tuna cones with me and go calm your nerves?"

Jim backed out of the room, sweat glistening on his bald head.

Richard sighed. "I hope he can pull himself together before the clients arrive."

"Is he sick?" Kate asked, nibbling the edge of a cone.

"Who knows?" Richard waved a hand in the air. "He's always got some drama. If it's not with his flying squirrel, it's with something else."

I'd had several encounters with Jim's flying squirrel, Rocky, and could attest to the level of crazy he could add to a situation.

I swallowed the last bite of the tuna cone, tasting the heat of the spices and washing it down with the remaining drops of my Fleur de Lis. I dabbed at my lips with a pink linen cocktail napkin.

"I'm going to pop into the ladies room before Debbie and Darla arrive."

"Don't take too long," Kate said. "You know it takes all of us to handle those two."

I walked back into the foyer and down the hall, passing the bathroom and pushing my way through the swinging door into the kitchen. A waiter in a black tuxedo passed me as he headed out of the kitchen, giving me a curious look, and I spotted Jim with his hands on the black marble counter taking long breaths. A chef wearing a white jacket and hat stood next to the stove, plating up hors d' oeuvres, and the air smelled of freshly baked bread.

"Are you okay?" I asked.

Jim jumped when he heard my voice, and his eyes grew wide. "I'm fine. A little tired is all."

"Are you sure it isn't something else?" I stepped closer to him. "You seemed startled when you heard me mention Cher Noble's murder."

He flinched. "I didn't know she'd been murdered. It was a bit of a shock to find out."

"Did you know her?" I asked.

Jim glanced around him. "I knew *of* her more than anything."

"I didn't know you were hooked into the DC drag scene."

He shook his head. "I'm not." He dropped his voice. "But some of the other waiters are."

I matched the volume of his voice. "Are you saying some other waiters at Richard Gerard Catering have connections to Cher?"

He bit his thumbnail. "The reason I remember Cher's name so well is because I heard so much about her when she won the DC drag races last year."

"The drag races?" I asked.

"Every Halloween in Dupont Circle, the drag queens in the city have a foot race in full heels and costumes. It's a pretty big deal."

I could imagine. "And the waiters here were friends with Cher?"

He gave a quick shake of his head. "One of them hated Cher because she beat him. He claims she cheated and complained about it for weeks."

I felt my pulse quicken. "Which waiter?"

"He's working with me today. His name is David."

I remembered the tuxedoed waiter who'd passed me when I entered the kitchen. "So would you say David still holds a grudge against Cher?"

"That diva cheated me out of my trophy," the sandy-haired waiter said from the doorway. "But she still can't hold a candle to Blanche Davidian."

CHAPTER 10

I stared at the waiter as he stepped into the kitchen and let the swinging door shut behind him. "Who's Blanche Davidian?"

The waiter threw back his shoulders and batted his blue eyes at me. "Me, of course. Well, Blanche is my drag name. I don't think Cher knows me as David."

As I looked at the preening waiter with his high cheekbones and long lashes, I didn't have a hard time imagining him dressed in drag. A part of me wondered if he had on fake lashes now.

"Knew you," I corrected.

David, aka Blanche, set his tray on the granite countertop. "What?"

"Cher Noble is dead," Jim said, his voice cracking. "She was strangled at yesterday's wedding."

David staggered back, his mouth dropping open. "How horrible. I had no idea."

From his reaction, either he was an exceptional actor or Cher's death really was news to him. I handed him a flute of champagne off a nearby silver tray. "You seem upset. I thought you hated Cher."

David threw back the entire glass in a single gulp. "We were rivals in the drag world, and things can get a little catty sometimes, but that doesn't mean I wanted her dead."

The chef opened the oven doors and pulled out two cookie sheets filled with golden brown puffed-up pastries. Both Jim and David jumped a bit as the metal sheets clattered against the cooling racks. I didn't recognize the bite-sized hors d'oeuvres, although the buttery scent reminded me I hadn't eaten breakfast, and I wondered if this was one of Richard's special carousel-themed creations.

I eyed David as he slumped against the counter. "Did either of you work yesterday's wedding?"

Jim shook his head. "I worked all of Richard's corporate events during the week so I was off."

"I was supposed to, but I went home sick about an hour into load in." David rubbed his forehead. "Richard read me the riot act about it, too."

"So Richard can attest to the fact you left early?" I asked.

"I'm sure he remembers yelling at me, and I know the other waiters overheard him." David raised an eyebrow. "Richard can get a little high-strung during weddings."

He didn't have to tell me. I'd had to talk my friend off the ledge when the wrong teaspoons had been delivered or the napkins weren't hemstitched.

David shook his head. "Why was Cher at the wedding in the first place? She wasn't on our staff."

"She was performing the wedding ceremony," I said.

David's face darkened. "I was the one who told her how to get approved by the DC courts to do weddings. That queen was always trying to upstage me."

The kitchen door flew open, banging against the wall, and we all spun around.

Richard stood holding the door with one arm and his other

hand on his hip. "So this is where my staff is hiding." His eyes shifted to me. "Annabelle, what are you doing?"

I reached for one of the highball glasses of water on the champagne tray. "Grabbing a glass of water. I didn't want to bother Jim since I was so close to the kitchen anyway."

Richard narrowed his eyes as if he didn't believe me. "Buster and Mack have arrived with the flowers, and the clients will be here soon, so if you're done distracting my paid employees . . ."

"Sorry," I muttered, casting a final look at Jim and David as I let Richard wave me out of the kitchen.

Richard caught me by the elbow after the kitchen door closed. "What were you really doing in there?"

"Did you send David home from the wedding yesterday?" I answered his question with one of my own.

"I didn't have a choice. He claimed to have a twenty-four-hour stomach virus, although I have a feeling he was really hungover." He sighed. "It's so hard to find good, attractive help these days."

"Have you ever considered not making physical attractiveness a prerequisite?"

Richard gave me a scandalized look. "If you're suggesting I hire waiters with dad bods, you can bite your tongue."

"There's a happy medium between dad bod and male model, you know."

"Richard Gerard Catering has a reputation for exceptional food served by exceptionally good-looking people. The world may have been taken over by millennial slackers, but I refuse to lower my standards."

I jerked a thumb in the direction of the kitchen. "I've got news for you. Your pretty boy waiters are all millennials."

Richard opened his mouth to respond then closed it again.

"Annabelle." Mack poked his head into the hall. "We need your opinion about the flowers."

I left Richard in the hall, spluttering about the technical age range of the millennial generation while I joined Mack in the tasting room. A tightly packed garland of pale-pink carnations had been swagged around the top of the table's canopy, and Buster balanced on a tall stepladder attaching a large white feather plume to the head of the gold carousel horse.

"Carnations?" Richard asked as he entered the room behind me.

Buster held up a hand from his precarious position on the top of the ladder. "I knew you were going to say something, but hear us out. You know we'd never use carnations as a filler flower, but when used in mass like this, you can hardly tell they're carnations."

Richard wrinkled his nose. "I could tell from a mile away blindfolded."

"I don't mind so much," Kate said, tapping her high heel on the hardwood floor. "We use peonies and roses so often, it's nice to throw another flower in the mix."

"Exactly what we thought." Mack threw a beefy arm around her shoulder, and the chains on his leather jacket jingled. "It's something different."

"So I suppose today is the day you all take leave of your senses?" Richard asked. "First Annabelle suggested I hire ugly waiters and now this?" He lowered his voice to a near hiss. "Carnations?"

I put up a finger. "First of all, I did not suggest ugly waiters; I only floated the idea of not insisting every waiter be able to moonlight as a Chippendale dancer."

Kate's eyes grew big. "Do you have Chippendale dancers on your staff?"

Richard glared at me. "Not if Annabelle has her way."

"Ridiculous," I muttered to myself, turning to Richard. "When have I ever had a say in who you hire? The same hires who've been known to unleash flying squirrels on my events, I might add."

Richard's face became a mottled shade of pink, and he sunk onto the couch and began fanning himself with both hands. "Do you think other planners know about the flying squirrel incidents?"

"It isn't like we have other planners attend our events," Kate said, sitting down next to him and patting his knee. "Has Rocky ever made an appearance when you've worked with other wedding planners? Maybe Brides by Brianna or T Pink?"

"Bite your tongue," Richard said to her. "You know I would never work with those hacks."

"Do you mean Tina Pink?" Mack asked as he held the step stool while Buster descended.

"How do you know her already?" I asked. "She's only been in business a few weeks."

Buster frowned as he stroked a hand down his dark goatee. "She sent us an email asking us to send her leads before she even left Melody's Mitzvahs."

"We didn't even know who she was," Mack added. "It was pretty bold. Why would we kick leads over to someone who's never even inquired with us before?"

"She should call herself Tina Tacky," Richard said. "Especially since she's hanging around Brianna."

Buster made a low growling noise in his throat. "Another reason to never work with her. It sounds like those two were made for each other."

It was no secret Buster and Mack despised Brianna after she'd told everyone she thought their floral design business, Lush, was overpriced and too fussy. Mention of her name was the only time I saw the Christian bikers get close to using profanity.

Mack patted Buster's shoulder. "Remember what Pastor Bruiser said about praying through the anger."

Buster nodded but his lips remained pressed together. I assumed to keep himself from saying what he really felt about the two awful planners.

"Well, I don't have to pray through the anger," Kate said. "I hope their fake blond hair turns green and falls out."

Mack giggled. "I would pray for that."

"Yoo hoo!" The warbly voice of Darla carried from the front door. "We're here."

I could smell the familiar scent of expensive perfume and top-shelf spirits heralding Debbie and Darla's arrival. Richard sprang from the couch and rushed to meet her, as Buster folded the stepladder with a snap and tucked it behind the fabric draped over the walls. I joined Richard in the hall to greet the mother-daughter duo and tried not to act surprised when I saw our formerly bubbly bride Debbie in a somber gray maternity dress with a protruding baby bump. Her mother, Darla, was as smiling and gushy as ever, but Debbie looked like she'd had all the wind let out of her sails and all the blush scrubbed off her cheeks.

The mother-daughter duo still both wore their hair in head-bands, but for the first time ever, I could see Debbie's dark roots. I suspected she couldn't color her hair because of the pregnancy and wondered if this was one of the reasons for her dour expression.

Debbie clutched my hand when she saw me. "Turner won't let me touch a drop of alcohol."

That explained her mood. Debbie, along with her boozy mother, had drunk her way through the wedding planning process. I didn't think I'd ever seen her sober before, although it was clear her mother was not.

"I'm having to drink for both of us," Darla said, throwing her head back in a loud laugh.

Debbie squeezed my hand tighter. "I think I might have to kill her."

"You don't mean that." I tried to laugh, but it came out sounding choked.

"Do you have any idea what it's like to be the only person not drinking all the time?" Debbie asked.

Actually, I knew exactly how it felt since Kate and I were often the only people not hammered, along with the rest of the staff, at the end of a wedding. It wasn't always fun being sober when everyone else was three sheets to the wind.

"You don't have long to go, do you?" I asked, looking down at her belly.

She let out a sigh. "Three months. But if this baby is even one day late, I'm inducing."

"Why don't we take a look at the decor ideas?" Kate asked as Darla leaned on her arm for support and, I suspected, to keep from falling over. Even from here I could smell bourbon on her breath.

Richard led the way into the tasting room, and both women gasped when they entered.

"It's perfect," Darla said. "Even prettier than I imagined."

Debbie beamed. "The gold carousel horse is the perfect touch of bling." She twisted to face Buster and Mack. "I love it."

Buster and Mack both visibly relaxed at the praise.

"Should we tell them the idea we had on the way here?" Darla asked, bouncing up and down on the balls of her feet.

"It was your idea," Debbie said, rolling her eyes. "You should tell them."

Darla either ignored her daughter's disdain or was too soused to notice. "Do you remember how we wanted to have decorative miniature ponies at the cocktail hour for Debbie's wedding?"

"I remember we couldn't because livestock regulations in DC museums prohibit it," Richard said.

We also nixed the idea of the ponies because tiny ponies were notorious ankle nippers, and the last thing we'd wanted at the wedding was a Bactine station for injured guests. Not to mention the inevitable pony poop on the museum's marble floors. I may have had to do a lot of odd things as a wedding planner, but I drew the line at scooping pony poo.

"Well, we don't have to worry about that since the shower is at my home," Darla continued. "I thought we could dress the ponies up like carousel horses and have them circulate throughout the house with hors d'oeuvres displayed on their saddles."

I watched the varying emotions as they crossed Richard's face. I couldn't identify all of them, but I knew horror and disgust were two of the major ones.

Kate stifled a laugh behind her hand, and I nudged her hard.

"Although I do adore the idea," I said, reaching out and pinching Richard on the arm before he could interrupt. "We need to have waiters serve the food in case guests ask about allergies. It's a safety issue."

Darla formed her mouth into a pout. "What about having the ponies without the food on their backs?"

"Why don't we have them on your lawn as people arrive?" Kate suggested.

It wasn't the worst idea, but I knew who was getting pony poop duty on the day of the shower.

"Like the swans in *Father of the Bride*." Darla clapped her hands. "But how can we make the cocktail area festive without the ponies?"

"Buster and I will create a massive floral carousel horse for your foyer," Mack said, throwing his arms open wide and jingling as he did so.

"Only one horse?" Darla said. "Our foyer is pretty large."

The entry hall of their Potomac McMansion was large enough to hold my entire apartment inside.

"We could do a pair of horses," Buster said.

"Or an entire carousel," Mack said, drawing a sharp look from Buster.

Debbie's face lit up. "An entire carousel made of flowers would be incredible. Can you really do it?"

Mack said yes, but I could see the crease between Buster's eyes as he thought about how exactly they would pull it off.

I felt my phone vibrate in the pocket of my dress and pulled it out as Richard showed Debbie and Darla to their seats to begin the tasting. I glanced at the text message on the screen.

"That can't be right," I muttered, looking at the message again.

"What's up?" Kate asked when she noticed me hanging back.

"I got a message from Reese." I touched my hand to my now-twitching eyelid. "Apparently, Fern turned himself in to the police."

CHAPTER 11

"I would ask if you could drive any faster but I'm afraid I might throw up." I pressed my palms to the roof of Kate's car as we took a turn onto Massachusetts Avenue without slowing.

"The only way I could get us there faster would be to ignore all the lights," Kate said. "Of course, if we had portable sirens to use on our cars, this wouldn't be a problem."

Kate and I had often thought wedding planners should be allowed to use detachable sirens we could slap on the top of our cars in case of wedding day emergencies.

"I wish the tasting hadn't taken so long," I said. "Meetings with Debbie and Darla used to go much quicker."

Kate honked her horn as a car braked in front of us. "Now that Debbie's sober, she's actually paying attention and asking questions. It really slows things down."

"Plus, Richard was so pleased with all his carousel-themed food he insisted on giving each item a royal introduction." I slammed my own foot on a nonexistent brake as Kate swerved around a car making a left turn.

"I half expected herald trumpeters to come out instead of waiters."

I cut my eyes to her. "Don't you dare give him that idea."

She laughed as she hooked a right onto a more residential street. "I could have done without the quinoa corn dogs. No corn dog should be that healthy. I could have eaten a dozen of the caramel apple pie pops, though."

I recognized the District Two police station ahead on our left and let out a breath, relieved we'd made it in one piece and without me being sick all over her car. I did not want to experience the quinoa corn dogs a second time. Kate angled her car into a street space, and I had the car door open before she'd turned off the engine.

The District Two station, headquarters for the officers who covered a section of northwest DC including Georgetown and reaching up past the National Cathedral to the border with Maryland, was a brown two-level building with a dated boxy design and dark windows. Mature trees shaded the lawn, the grass green and brown in patches.

"So how are we going to play this?" Kate asked as I walked around the car to join her.

"I'm hoping we don't have to play anything." I hiked my black purse onto my shoulder. "We're here to pick up Fern. It should be cut and dry."

Kate fluffed her hair. "You know what they say about the best played plans of mice and men."

I rolled the expression over in my head for a moment. "You mean the best *laid* plans?"

Kate frowned. "That doesn't sound right."

I sighed and led the way up the paved walk toward the glass double doors, with Kate hurrying behind me in her heels. I pushed open one side and held it for Kate as she entered, her shoes clip-clopping on the tile floor. We approached the front desk to our right but it was unmanned.

"Is that Fern?" Kate asked, pointing behind the desk and beyond a glass divider to where a group of officers gathered, some sitting on the edges of wooden desks and others standing.

I observed Fern, wearing a pale-blue seersucker suit, wrap a black tie around an officer's neck.

"There are so many more stylish ways to knot a tie," he said. "Personally, I like the look of the Eldridge, but I don't think it works with the severe cut of your uniform, so I'm going to show you how to do a full Windsor."

"Is he giving them fashion advice?" Kate whispered to me.

"It looks like it, but there's always the possibility we've passed into a different dimension." I took out my phone and sent off a quick text to Reese telling him I was at the station.

Kate snapped her fingers. "That actually makes more sense."

Reese appeared from the back of the group of officers and walked over to us, his eyes wide. "You've got to get him out of here."

I put one hand on my hip. "I thought you were the one who insisted he come down to the station for questioning."

He pulled me to the side so the other officers couldn't see us as easily. He put one hand on my waist and leaned close, brushing his lips across my cheek. "Babe, you've got to help me out here."

I felt my pulse quicken and my cheeks warm. I cleared my throat and pointed to Kate who still stood only a few feet away from us.

"Don't mind me," she said when Reese glanced at her. "I'm learning how to make a Windsor knot."

"We'll take him with us," I said. "But I thought you needed to know his connection to Cher Noble and any clues he might have."

Reese stole a glance at his watch. "He's been here for two hours. He told me everything he knew in the first ten minutes, and since then he's turned the Metropolitan Police into the Fashion Police."

"So tie knotting is not his first tutorial?" I heard a round of applause as Fern finished his Windsor knot and watched as he took a series of bows.

Reese crossed his arms. "He's already taught my female officers how to jazz up their uniform with scarves and explained why our department-issued slacks add fifteen pounds. Half the department is about to go on a diet, and the other half is on the verge of some serious comfort eating."

I pressed my lips together to keep from laughing.

"Don't you dare laugh," Reese warned, his own mouth twitching at the sides.

"Was Fern's information helpful at least?" I asked once I'd gotten myself under control. "He knew Cher better than any of us."

"He told us about Cher's concerns about being stalked and about the tire slashing, but since Cher never told him why or who she thought could be behind it, we don't have much to go on."

"I actually found out something useful," I said. "One of Richard's waiters had an ongoing feud with the victim."

Reese gave me a stern look. "What did we say about you getting involved in the case?"

I held up my hands in mock surrender. "I promised I wouldn't meddle in any more criminal investigations, and I meant it. This bit of information happened to fall into my lap. The waiter was at the tasting I came from, and he told me he held a grudge against Cher for beating him at the Halloween drag races. He claims Cher cheated him out of the trophy."

"Back up. You think another drag queen strangled our victim over a foot race trophy?"

When he put it like that, it didn't sound like such a great lead. "I didn't say I thought he did it, but he did know Cher, had a problem with her, and was at the wedding."

"He was at the scene of the crime?" Reese took his notebook out of his blazer pocket. "That changes things. What's this waiter's name?"

"David. I don't know his real last name. Richard does. I know his drag name is Blanche Davidian."

Reese raised an eyebrow but didn't comment.

"He claims he left the wedding before Cher was killed or even arrived," I said. "He's adamant Richard sent him home and a dozen people witnessed it."

Reese tapped his pen against his notebook. "That doesn't mean he actually left. Unless he can prove otherwise, it's possible he could have returned to Meridian House after pretending to leave. There are lots of places to hide outside the house."

"So you're going to follow up on my lead?" I asked, rocking back on my heels.

He grinned at me. "I hate to admit it, but it's the best one we have so far. The crime scene had about a thousand fingerprints since so many people were in and out of the house. None of the tests for fibers found on the body have come back. The autopsy showed what we knew at the site. The victim was garroted and the feather boa wrapped around her neck. There were no prints on the victim except her own and no skin under her fingernails, so the killer probably wore gloves."

I shivered a little as I thought about Cher Noble lying dead on the floor. "Why would there be skin under her fingernails?"

"If someone was choking you from behind, wouldn't you reach around and claw at them?" Reese raised his hands behind his neck to demonstrate. "If the killer had bare hands or bare arms, chances are good the victim would have scratched them and had skin under her nails."

"Cher Noble was a big girl," I said. "Whoever killed her also had to be pretty tall and strong."

Reese nodded. "I doubt a woman could have done this. Or most men."

"Then I'm not sure Blanche Davidian is your guy. He isn't as tall or broad as Cher."

"It's still the best lead we've got," Reese said. "And this Blanche could know more about Cher's possible enemies."

"I'm glad I could help, and I'm glad you can admit I helped."

Reese tucked a loose strand of hair behind my ear. "I'll admit you single-handedly solved the case if you promise to take Fern out of here."

I looked over to Fern as he unfurled a black smock over an officer's beefy shoulders. Did he keep a stylists' smock on himself at all times?

"Don't worry, sweetie," Fern said to the visibly nervous officer. "We're going to have this comb-over taken care of in no time flat."

"Kate," I said. "It's time for us to go and take Fern with us."

"Before he fixes the comb-over?" she asked, gesturing at the candy floss hair the man had styled up and over his bald head. "I feel like Fern is doing a public service with this one."

I looked at Reese. "Before or after the comb-over?"

Reese paused. "After. That comb-over has driven me crazy for years."

Fern looked up, spotted us, and beamed. "Annabelle! Kate! I'm thinking about opening a satellite salon right here in the station. Go where there's the most need. What do you think?"

Reese groaned. "I think I need to put in for a transfer."

CHAPTER 12

"Finally," I said as I dropped my purse on the floor of my apartment and sank onto the couch, kicking my shoes off and crinkling my toes into the area carpet.

The fading sunlight cast a warm glow from the windows, and I followed the light as it moved across the floor, illuminating the dust bunnies and reminding me I needed to clean. I leaned my head back and closed my eyes so I could soak in the silence. After a long day including a dramatic tasting with Debbie and Darla and dragging Fern out of the police station while he was mid-makeover, I was glad for the solace. I hadn't had a moment alone since the murder, and I needed it more than I'd known. Now the only thing I wanted was to get out of my clothes and into bed.

I sat up, scooped up my shoes, and headed for my bedroom, removing the elastic and shaking out my hair as I walked. Since I'd slept on my couch the night before, my bed was still made and topped with a stack of ecru embroidered pillows I usually tossed to the floor. I put my shoes on the floor of my closet and slipped out of my dress, tossing it into my bright-yellow dry-cleaning bag. The bag bulged at the sides, and I made a mental note to drop it off before I found myself without a little black dress to wear to the next wedding. I pulled on yoga pants and a Wedding Belles T-shirt and smoothed my hair up into another high ponytail. Now this was more like it. Even though I had to spend most of my time in dresses or suits, wash-and-wear clothes with a healthy amount of Lycra were more my style.

Despite the multi-course tasting I'd sat through at lunchtime, I felt the first twinges of hunger. I reminded myself the courses had been bite-sized, and it was now dark outside as I went to my kitchen to assess my options. I sighed as I looked in the fridge. A few cans of soda, some aging Thai takeout, condiments, and a bottle of unopened bubbly courtesy of Richard, who always kept me stocked up with what he considered the essentials.

"Pathetic," I mumbled to no one as I made a beeline for my purse and the phone tucked inside. I paused for a moment, staring at my speed dial options and debating between pizza and Chinese. Before I could dial, the phone began trilling. I saw Reese's name on the screen and answered.

"I owe you one," he said.

I laughed. "For convincing Fern not to open a salon inside your precinct? Yes, you do. He'd convinced himself fixing your fellow officers' bad hair was a calling akin to Mother Teresa attending to the lepers."

Reese's deep chuckle made my heart beat a little faster.

"I was about to order Chinese if you're interested."

"Tempting," he said. "You more than the Chinese, but I still have a mound of paperwork, and I finally got the security footage from Meridian House."

"They have cameras?" I'd never noticed them and wondered if they were hidden behind tapestries or in the eyes of portraits.

"Some strategically placed ones. I'm hoping one of them will give us a glimpse of the killer either coming or going."

"Good luck," I said.

"How about dinner tomorrow night?" Reese asked.

"Should I order extra takeout tonight?" I asked.

"I won't subject you to two nights of Chinese takeout," he said. "Dinner out. Think of someplace you'd like to go."

I smiled. A real date. "Sounds good."

"See you tomorrow, babe," he said before disconnecting.

I couldn't stop grinning as I pulled up my speed dial takeout option again. Now I was really hungry. I was about to speed dial Kitchen Number 1 when there was a sharp rap on my door.

"You've got to be kidding." I got up to answer the door, cracking it a bit to reveal Leatrice in a beige trench coat belted over flannel cow-print pajamas.

"I'm so glad you're home." She looked behind her as if she was being followed. "Can I come in?"

I let her in and looked out in the empty hallway once more before closing the door. "Is everything okay? Did you see someone suspicious?"

She shook her head. "I'm keeping an eye out for the pizza guy. He still has five minutes to get it here before it's late."

"Don't let me keep you." I started to open the door again. "You might miss him if you're up here."

She waved a hand to dismiss my concern. "I gave them your address."

Of course she did. Why hadn't I guessed in the first place? I closed the door and put my phone on the coffee table, giving up the idea of eating Chinese takeout. "What kind of pizza?"

"Hawaiian," Leatrice said. "I'm trying to eat more exotic foods."

I flopped down on the couch. "I don't know if I'll be good company. It's been a long day."

"I know what you mean. Making a citizen's arrest yesterday really took it out of me." She bit the edge of her pink bottom lip, getting lipstick on her teeth. "How is Fern anyway?"

"He's fine. He's decided to forgive you for tackling him."

"That's good news." Leatrice touched a hand to her platinum blond hairdo. "I was hoping he'd help me with my roots."

"Since he's the one who took you blond, it's probably fair he helps you maintain it." As I looked at Leatrice, I couldn't help thinking this is what it would look like if Mary Tyler Moore and Marilyn Monroe had morphed then spent a few days in a food dehydrator.

"I do like being a blonde." Leatrice giggled. "It's true what they say about having more fun. You should try it, Annabelle."

I shook my head. "I can barely maintain the beauty regimen I have now. No way I could do touch-ups every six weeks. I'd look like a skunk in no time flat."

"I'm surprised not to see the detective here." Leatrice scanned my living room. "Unless he's hiding in the back."

"Nope," I said, hoping she wouldn't notice the color I could feel creeping up my neck. "No detective."

"Was he upset I did his job for him?" Leatrice asked. "I didn't mean to step on any toes."

"He still had plenty of leads to follow," I said. "I don't think he was upset."

I didn't tell her Reese had almost burst out laughing and had to leave the room to compose himself when she'd dragged Fern upstairs in plastic handcuffs and announced she'd made a citizen's arrest.

"Do they have any suspects aside from Fern?"

"Fern isn't actually a suspect," I said. "He was a witness and had information about the case."

Leatrice's face fell. "So I probably won't be receiving a reward from the police department for apprehending a suspect?"

"Doubtful," I told her as Richard's number popped up on the screen, and I answered.

"Am I to understand you turned one of my waiters in to the police?" His voice registered somewhere between shrill and hysterical.

"That's not what happened." I sat down on the couch, resigned to the fact I wouldn't be eating for a while.

"Really? Because I got a call from your boy toy asking me to confirm the whereabouts of David on the wedding day. He said you told him I'd sent David home early and his connection to Cher."

"Did I lie?" I asked, ignoring his use of the phrase "boy toy."

"No," Richard spluttered, "but that's hardly the point, is it?"

"Isn't it? If David is innocent, won't you telling Reese what happened on the wedding day clear him faster? His connection to Cher would have come out eventually." I propped up my bare feet on the glass coffee table. "I thought you wanted the police to find who murdered Cher."

Leatrice perched on the chair across from me, making no secret of listening in on my conversation.

"Of course I do." Richard's voice softened. "But do you have to decimate my business to do it?"

"One waiter being questioned is hardly decimating your business."

"David isn't the only waiter who knew Cher," Richard said, the words coming out in a rush.

I sat up and dropped my feet to the floor. "What? How many more knew her, and how many were working the wedding?"

Leatrice's garishly pink mouth made a perfect O.

Richard sighed. "I don't know for sure, but Cher was well-known in the drag world, and David isn't our only cater waiter who moonlights in a dress."

"I had no idea DC had such a big drag community," I said.

"With this many uptight people in pinstripe suits?" Richard laughed. "Darling, it's a given."

I trusted Richard to know the ins and outs of the city better than I did. He was a native of the capital, while I'd only been here for seven years.

"You need to give this information to the police," I said. "I'm sure Reese will handle it discreetly."

Richard gave a snort on the other end of the line. "Do I need to remind you of the time he shut my business down and made me his number one suspect in a poisoning? It took my business months to recover."

"You mean the time you operated your business illegally out of my kitchen and almost got me in trouble with the cops as well?"

Richard remained silent for a moment. "A long memory is less attractive on you than it is on me, Annabelle."

"As are most things," I said.

"Well aren't you sweet?" Richard said. "I have to admit your fashion sense has improved tremendously under my tutelage."

Richard's "tutelage" consisted of horrified looks, gasps of disapproval, and refusals to be seen with me until I changed clothes.

"So are you going to tell Reese or should I?" I asked over a loud rapping on my door.

Leatrice leapt up and answered it, taking the pizza and handing the money to the delivery guy in less than a minute.

"Depends. Is he at your door?"

"No. It was the pizza guy. The only person in my apartment is Leatrice."

"Really? I would offer to come over, but I feel like I've had my Leatrice quotient for the day."

"Haven't we all?" I said as Leatrice dropped the pizza box on the coffee table and hopped onto the couch, tucking her legs underneath her. The smell of cheese and grease filled the air and made my stomach growl.

"I suppose I'm going to call your boyfriend and give him even more reasons to come after me," Richard said. "If you don't hear from me tomorrow, you might want to check the city jail."

Always the drama queen. I was surprised Richard didn't have an alter ego like Cher Noble or Blanche Davidian. The thought made me wonder.

"You don't have a drag persona, do you?" I asked.

The phone disconnected, and Richard was gone. Had he heard me, or had he already hung up before I asked my question? I shook my head. If Richard dressed in drag I would know, wouldn't I? I was his best friend after all.

"Richard in drag?" Leatrice wrinkled her already-wrinkled nose. "I wonder what he'd look like as a blonde."

I shook the disturbing thought of Richard in a platinum wig out of my head and took a bite of Hawaiian pizza.

CHAPTER 13

I stood on Columbia Road and looked across the street at the two-level cream-colored building. It was fronted with tall round-top windows and a black awning extending from the door on the right. I tilted my head back and noticed the railing around the rooftop patio and the string lights draped from a center pole to create a canopy. Since it was daytime, the string lights weren't on, and the patio was empty except for the tall ficus trees positioned at the corners.

"Are you sure it's open?" I locked my car with a click of the remote after Kate and Fern joined me on the sidewalk. I took a final sip of my now lukewarm mocha, cringing as I swallowed the dregs of the drink, and glanced around for a trash can.

I'd only been to Perry's, the restaurant famous for its drag queen brunch on Sunday and its rooftop sushi happy hour, once before. When Kate and I had come with our grooms, the lines had been out the door, and you could hear the pulsating music down the block. This quiet, almost somber, building seemed like an entirely different place.

"It's not open to the public." Fern smoothed the front of his black suit, his enormous blue topaz ring catching the sun. "This is a friends-only memorial reception for Cher Noble."

"So why are we here?" I asked Kate.

My assistant had chosen her most modest dress, a black V-neck sheath, but it still didn't come close to her knees. Luckily, I'd been able to find one black dress in my closet not in need of dry cleaning. Unfortunately, it was the dress I rarely wore because I felt it was too short, so, for once, my hemline wasn't much longer than Kate's.

"To support Fern." Kate patted his arm.

"Then why am I here?" Richard asked, walking up from where he'd parked a few cars down from us. "Can't two people do as good a job as three?"

I linked my arm through Richard's, glad he wasn't wearing linen today, although the fabric of his beige suit felt expensive per usual. "You know you wouldn't miss this."

Richard shifted his crossbody leather bag, and Hermes poked his tiny black-and-brown head out from under the flap. He yipped when he saw us, and I gave Richard a look.

"What? I couldn't leave him at home. I'm going to be gone all day. Anyway, Hermes is a supremely well-behaved dog. More well-behaved than most people I know." Richard closed the flap, and Hermes wedged his head so only his nose and eyes were visible. "No one will even notice."

Fern rubbed Hermes's nose. "Maybe he can help us sniff out the killer. Dogs are intuitive."

"He's a Yorkie, not a hunting dog," Richard said. "Unless the killer is covered in treats, I'm not sure Hermes will be much help. And are you still going on about us solving the murder?"

"You all promised to find out who killed Cher," Fern said, adjusting the white silk flower he'd pinned to his lapel. "This will be the perfect place to talk to people who knew her and gather information."

"Did I promise?" Richard asked, shaking his head. "As the voice of reason in this group, I'm sure I made no such promise."

There was no point in telling Fern I had also not promised to solve Cher's murder and had actually promised Reese I wouldn't get involved—a promise I intended to keep. I also decided not to mention how much Fern's silk flower boutonniere made him look like an undertaker. For all I knew, it was the look he was going for.

Fern threw his hand up to stop traffic as he barreled across the intersection toward the restaurant, and the rest of us hurried behind him. When we reached the other side, I dropped my empty paper coffee cup in a black steel trash can and rushed to catch up as Fern disappeared inside the double doors under the black awning.

I sighed as I stepped through the door, hearing the sounds of jazz from above and eyeing the tall staircase leading to the second-floor restaurant.

"This had better be worth it," Richard muttered behind me.

When we reached the top, I looked across the open floor plan with its pumpkin-colored walls and sleek black curtains framing the long windows overlooking the street. A bar ran along one wall, and a collection of shiny blue tiles covered another. Most of the tables had been pushed to the side, but the blue-and-orange couches by the windows remained. An antique fireplace, painted black and inset with a mirror, was tucked into a corner, its mantle crowded with framed photographs of Cher Noble. I did a double take when I realized the area in front of the blue-tile wall usually reserved for the buffet table now featured a hot-pink casket with an arrangement of brightly colored flowers perched on faux marble columns on each side. A wall of gold velvet fabric had been erected in front of the casket but was pulled back and tied with tassels.

"Who knew caskets came in pink?" I whispered to Kate as a husky woman in a flapper-style red dress passed us.

"You don't think Cher's body is in there, do you?" Kate whispered back as she led the way through the crowd of garishly dressed mourners, their hands filled with equally colorful cocktails.

I shook my head. "The last I heard the coroner hadn't released it yet."

"It's ceremonial." Fern paused as we drew close to the casket and dabbed his eyes with an eyelet lace handkerchief. "But it makes quite the centerpiece for the party, don't you think?"

I, for one, had never thought about using a casket as a focal point for an event, but Wedding Belles didn't dabble in funerals or wakes. Although, with our current track record, it might not be such a bad marketing plan.

"It's a little too much." Richard made a face. "Especially setting it out where the buffet usually is. I'm afraid at any second they're going to plop some platters of food on top."

Fern recognized one of the drag queens in attendance and stepped away to talk to her. Hermes extended his head further out of Richard's bag and sniffed the air. I didn't blame him. The air was thick with the smell of food—not surprising for a restaurant —but I couldn't see any stations or waiters. Although it was still morning, the plain toast I'd had earlier left me eager for lunch.

"I'm going to hunt down the food," Richard said. As a caterer, he couldn't help assessing the cuisine at any party.

"Try not to be too judgmental," I said. "This is a reception for the deceased."

Richard smoothed his pastel-pink tie. "Annabelle, you wound me. When have I ever been critical of someone else's event?"

I fought the urge not to remind him of the last party we'd attended where a competing caterer had wrapped the ends of their baby lamb chops in tinfoil, and Richard had gotten so lightheaded he'd had to breathe into a paper bag for ten minutes. "Fine. But don't try to slip out without us."

"Right back at you," he said as he moved off through the crowd with Hermes bobbing in the bag beside him and sniffing at guests as they went.

A strolling jazz singer in a floor-length gray sequined dress held a purple microphone close to her lips as she belted out "Funny Valentine" in a warbling baritone. The rest of her band—tuxedoed men playing keyboard, bass, and drums—were set up by the windows. I ducked as the singer flung her arms wide at the end of the song.

"I see lots of cocktails." Kate indicated the colorful drinks everyone seemed to be holding. "But where are they coming from? It doesn't look like the regular bar is open."

"It's not even noon," I said. "Do you think the drinks are alcoholic?"

Kate cocked one eyebrow as a drag queen with a lemon yellow beehive and a five o'clock shadow passed by. "God, I hope so."

"I didn't know you'd be here," a tall blonde in a sparkly silver fringed dress said as she walked up to me.

I looked around. "Are you talking to me?"

The blonde leaned down, and her Farrah Fawcett hair spilled over her shoulders. "It's me. Blanche Davidian."

I reached for Kate, who had drifted a few feet away in her search for booze, and pulled her over. "This is the waiter I told you about. David, I mean Blanche Davidian."

Blanche took Kate's hand and kissed it. "Charmed, I'm sure."

Kate giggled, and I rolled my eyes. Even a man dressed in platform heels and a push-up bra could turn Kate into a marshmallow.

"I thought you and Cher were rivals," I said, studying Blanche's elaborately made-up face for any homicidal maniac tells. "So why come to a party celebrating her?"

"Guilt, I suppose," Blanche said.

My ears perked up. Were about to hear a murder confession?

"Not in the way you might think," Blanche said when she

looked at my expression. "I feel bad I made such a big deal about a stupid race. Cher was a legend in our world, and she didn't deserve to be murdered. I'm here to pay my respects like everyone else."

Kate rubbed Blanche's arm as the blonde sniffled into her spangled sleeve. I stood on my tiptoes to glimpse over the crowd. We'd lost Fern in the sea of people, and since most guests were taller than us and wore huge heels, it was impossible to spot him. I thought a man passing in a dark suit might be Fern, but I realized I was mistaken when I saw the man's hand. Fern would rather be the one in the casket than be seen in public wearing a pinky ring.

A woman in a powdered wig shuffled by, her dress a table extending out in a perfect circle holding an assortment of artfully displayed sushi. I considered a salmon roll before deciding it was a little too early to eat raw fish. I also wasn't sure how I felt about eating it off a person's outfit. Kate had no such "not before noon" or "no eating off a living statue" rules and plucked two California rolls from the living buffet.

I turned my attention back to Blanche. "Have you spoken to the police yet?"

"I promised the detective I'd stop by today after the reception," Blanche said. "Although I don't know how much I can tell them. I probably left the wedding before Cher even showed up."

"Did you drive home or take a taxi?" I asked.

"I walked. I don't live far from Meridian House."

I still wasn't convinced Blanche had actually left Meridian House when she claimed, but I nodded as if I believed her. "Any details you might have noticed could help the case. Maybe someone else who had a connection to Cher was at the house."

Blanche bit the edge of her fire-engine-red bottom lip. "Like I told you before, Cher and I weren't close. Plus, the house was a madhouse when I left. I must have seen a dozen people loading in as I was leaving. I saw you, those huge florists and all their crew, the hairdresser and the grooms, the girls in those gold dresses."

"Did any of them look sinister?" Kate asked.

Blanche's false eyelashes fluttered. "Why would anyone at the wedding look sinister?"

"Cher thought she was being stalked," Kate said in a low voice. "Her stalker might have come to the wedding to finish her off."

I shot Kate a look. So much for keeping that information on the down low.

Blanche sucked in air. "Stalked?" She narrowed her eyes at me. "Is this why the police want to talk to me? They think because Cher and I had a feud I would stalk and murder her?"

"No," I said. "They want to talk to you because you were at the wedding. They're talking to everyone who was there."

Blanche flipped a bouncy golden curl off her shoulder. "I hope you're right. I had nothing to do with Cher's death. Not only do I have an airtight alibi, I know someone who wanted her dead way more than I did."

I watched as Blanche flounced off into the crowd. "I wonder who she meant?"

CHAPTER 14

I took a pair of martini glasses filled with pale-pink liquid off a passing tray and handed one to my assistant. "I think we both need a drink."

Kate took a sip. "I'm assuming she'll tell Reese when she meets with him. I'd love to be a fly on the wall, especially if she wears the dress."

Richard walked up with a paper napkin filled with hors d'oeuvres he was feeding bite by bite to Hermes. "Who was the blonde who stormed away from you?"

"That's Blanche Davidian."

His face was blank.

"Your waiter, David. The one you sent home early on Saturday."

His eyes grew wide. "Really? I never would have pegged him as a blue eye shadow type of guy."

I scanned the crowd looking for Fern as I tasted the fruity cocktail I'd snagged. The gold velvet drapes were drawn over the casket, and a microphone had been moved in front. I wondered if people would start giving toasts soon. The jazz band kicked into a mournful version of "It Had To Be You," and I turned to see a new singer in teal chiffon with pink hair teased so high she had to duck to walk under the hanging light fixtures. While the other performer had been a baritone, this singer was a bass. I felt like I was listening to Barry White and watching Dame Edna. I listened to her, transfixed, until she began singing "The Lady is a Tramp."

"How long do you think we need to stay?" Richard asked. "I think I'm starting to lose my grip on reality."

"Let's get Fern and take off," I said.

I tried to peer over the heads, but mostly saw lots of big hair.

Kate nudged me. "Are those our grooms?"

I followed her line of sight, not exactly sure if I was up to facing Stefan so soon after the wedding. I saw Jesse in a dark suit moving through the crowd toward the antique fireplace, but not Stefan.

Kate raised her arm above the crowd and waved, calling out Jesse's name. He swung his head around and broke into a smile when he saw us. We wiggled our way over to him with me holding my drink high so it wouldn't be jostled, Richard mumbling about personal space, and Hermes giving the occasional yip.

Jesse gave us enthusiastic hugs when we reached him. "Can you believe we're seeing each other again so soon?"

"No, I can't," Richard said, shifting Hermes on his hip.

I shot him a look. "He means we aren't usually this lucky. Most of our couples run off on their honeymoon right away."

Jesse gave a tight laugh as he reached out and scratched Hermes's head. "You know Stefan. He had some work thing come up, so we're going to the Seychelles next week instead of right after the wedding. He made it up to me by getting us the Presidential Suite at The Wharf for this week."

Kate swiveled her head. "Where is Stefan?"

Jesse bobbed one shoulder up and down. "He said he was going to get us drinks, but he must have gotten lost."

I hoped he'd gotten lost. I had a feeling Stefan might want to rehash the wedding, and I was in no mood.

"We saw Fern a few minutes ago," Jesse said. "I had no idea he and Cher were friends."

"It was a surprise to all of us," I said, continuing to scan the crowd for Stefan, nervous he would appear at any minute and start complaining about the wedding.

"Speaking of Fern," Richard said in my ear, "weren't we going to find him and go?"

"We were actually on our way out." I squeezed Jesse's arm. "Please tell Stefan we were sorry we missed him."

I pulled Kate away after she gave Jesse a final hug. "Let's find Fern before Stefan finds us."

"Good thinking." Kate squatted down. "It's easier to look through the legs than try to see over the hair. There aren't many pant legs in here, anyway, so he shouldn't be too hard to spot." After a minute, she pointed. "Found him. His legs are on the move and headed toward the gold velvet."

We wiggled our way through the tightly packed mourners as they laughed and tossed back drinks. More than one cocktail splashed onto my arm, and I could feel my shoes sticking to the floor.

"Watch the suit, people," Richard cried behind me. "Beige does not hide spills."

Fern's face brightened when he saw us. "I wondered where you'd gone."

"Where we'd gone?" I said. "You left us in the dust."

He gave a wave of a hand. "I needed to find Hedda Lettuce." He gestured to a brunette in a one-shoulder canary-yellow cocktail dress that left little to the imagination but filled me with many questions. "She put this whole thing together."

"Hedda Lettuce?" Kate asked, glancing down at her empty martini glass. I suspected she was wondering if she'd had too many.

"Call me Hedda." She extended a perfectly manicured hand to both of us as she looked us up and down. "Aren't you dolls? I love the black. Very Audrey Hepburn." Her eyes fell on Richard and dropped to Hermes. "The dog goes perfectly with your suit, hon. Really adds a nice contrast."

Both Richard and Hermes seemed to preen from the compliment as they grinned at Hedda.

"You must have been close to Cher to do this." I shifted closer to Kate as a Marie Antoinette doppelganger passed by with a rolling metal frame skirt around her waist which held rows of champagne flutes all the way to the floor. This was officially the first party I'd attended where all the food displays were people powered.

Fern snagged one of the glasses of champagne off the human display. "Hedda knew Cher better than anyone. That's why she's going to kick off the tributes."

Hedda stepped up to the microphone before I could ask her what she knew about Cher's stalker.

"Give me a hand, girls," Fern said as he tugged back one side of the gold fabric.

Kate and I took the other side with me holding back the heavy fabric while Kate tied it with a thick gold tassel.

Richard stepped back and eyed the velvet. "It's not quite even."

"Where's the other tassel?" Fern asked as he stood with an armful of gold velvet.

I turned to look for it and noticed the pink casket behind me was now open with both halves of the lid propped up. "Odd. I thought this was for decor."

Kate grasped my arm. "Is that what I think it is?"

I spotted the end of the gold tassel hanging out of the casket at the same time I noticed a flash of silver from inside. I took a step closer, and Kate shuffled along behind me. I heard Hermes begin to growl in the background.

"I thought you said the coroner hadn't released the body," Kate said, hiding her face behind my shoulder.

"That's not Cher Noble," I said as I got a clear view into the casket and the body within. "It's Blanche Davidian."

CHAPTER 15

"There's the missing tassel," Fern cried, stepping closer to the open casket.

I turned around and tried to step in front of him. "Maybe we should leave the velvet down for a while." I dropped my voice and gave Kate a pointed look. "Like until you call 911."

She fumbled in her purse. "On it."

Richard's face froze as he alternately looked at the casket and down at Hermes, whose growl was a low rumble. "Is that . . .?"

Fern put his hands on his hips. "We can't have one side pulled up and the other side hanging down, Annabelle. You know how I hate asymmetry."

True. Fern had not been happy during the days of one-sided angled haircuts.

"I'll drop my side," I said, still blocking his way. I tried not to look at the body lying sprawled in the casket, but even from the corner of my eye I could tell it had not been a neat job. The body was twisted awkwardly, and the spangly silver dress was bunched up in the middle, almost like Blanche had been tossed inside.

Fern squinted at me as Hedda Lettuce turned from the microphone, waving us out of the way with one hand.

"Close the lid," she said, her voice a gravelly rumble.

Fern sidestepped me to reach the lid and screamed so loudly I had to cover my ears. I caught him as he staggered back and began to sway, his eyes fluttering before rolling back into his head. I braced myself under his dead weight but couldn't keep him from slipping down to the floor and landing at Kate's feet. Hermes leapt from Richard's bag to the inside of the casket where he began barking.

Richard staggered against the casket as Hermes scampered up and down on the corpse, yipping furiously.

Hedda gaped at Fern's limp form and glanced up at the casket. The microphone picked up her deep voice. "What is Blanche Davidian doing inside the casket?"

So much for keeping this quiet until the police arrived. Every person in the room stopped talking and looked up to where Kate and I stood in front of a hot-pink open casket with Fern lying at our feet and a dog barking on top of a dead body. I saw a few phone flashes go off.

"It looks like there's been an accident," I whispered to Hedda, hoping the mic wouldn't pick up my words.

"Accident?" Hedda took a few jerky steps toward the casket and paled under her heavy makeup. "Is she dead?"

I let my eyes wander to the body. The purple cast of the face and the protruding bloodshot eyes left little doubt Blanche Davidian was dead, and the gold tassel wrapped around her neck made it pretty clear she'd been murdered. I felt my stomach do a flip-flop as I looked at the dead drag queen and was glad I hadn't eaten the sushi. I scooped up Hermes and handed him to Richard, whose usually tan face looked several shades paler.

Hedda put her hands to her cheeks and shook her head. "Who could have done this?"

I didn't know what to say, and I didn't feel like I knew Hedda well enough to comfort her.

Fern stirred at my feet, pushing himself onto his hands and rubbing his head. "Why am I on the floor? What happened?"

Kate kneeled down next to him. "Maybe you should stay down there for a while."

He shook his head. "I'm getting dirt all over my suit." He got to his knees and clutched the side of the casket to pull himself up the rest of the way.

I stepped forward to stop him, but he'd already hoisted himself so his face was even with Blanche's. His eyes widened, he gave a squeak, and collapsed again.

"Let's hope he stays down this time," Kate said. She hooked her hands under his armpits and dragged him over to the tile wall, propping him so he looked like he was napping upright.

The crowd murmured behind us, and I heard sirens in the distance. I saw a few guests drift toward the staircase, including Jesse and Stefan. Luckily, Stefan wasn't looking in my direction, so I hoped he hadn't seen me. If I had to juggle a groomzilla and a dead drag queen for a second time I would lose my mind. I grabbed Richard's arm. "This is a crime scene. No one can leave until the police arrive."

He looked at me blankly, but Hermes yipped his agreement.

"We don't want Blanche's killer to escape, do we?" I asked.

Richard hoisted his dog higher in his arms. "Hermes and I will be at the stairs and make sure no one leaves."

I turned to Hedda. "Can you make an announcement to calm everyone down and make sure they don't run for the exit?"

She pressed her coral lips together and stepped up to the mic. "Forgive the technical difficulties, sweeties, but don't leave yet. We'll be raffling off a spa weekend in a few minutes."

The guests who'd been heading to the stairs stopped and turned around. I had to give it to Hedda, dangling a spa weekend in front of people was pretty ingenious.

"I hope we win," Kate said, nudging me. "That would turn this week around."

"Definitely." I didn't have the heart to tell her the getaway was a scam.

A pair of blue-uniformed police officers appeared at the top of the staircase, blocked by Richard who appeared to be asking for ID. Kate hurried over to them while I stayed with Hedda to block the other guests' view of the body.

Hedda handed me a glass of champagne from the live display who still stood nearby and took one herself. "Here, sweetie. You and I could both use a drink."

I thanked her and took a sip, the bubbly feeling oddly comforting as it cooled my throat. "Did you know Blanche well?"

Hedda tossed her hair back. "Not as well as I knew Cher, but she was still part of our community. It's no secret Blanche had issues with Cher, but I never thought of it as more than a spat."

Any theory of Blanche killing Cher had flown out the window, so I wasn't sure how their feud could have anything to do with either murder. Unless drag queens had factions and there was some Jets versus Sharks thing going on. Looking over the sequined and hairsprayed crowd, I doubted it.

Hedda drained her champagne and hiccupped. She clasped my hand. "I think I may have been one of the last people to see both victims before they died."

"What?"

"I haven't told anyone yet because I was too distraught, but I dropped Cher off at the wedding on Saturday. She was nervous about using her car after her tires were slashed, especially since she'd be in full drag, so she asked me to drop her off." Hedda dropped her eyes. "I was waiting for her call to come pick her up, but it never came."

"You need to tell this to the police," I said. "You might have seen something important without knowing it."

Hedda looked at me, her dramatically arched eyebrows furrowed. "Do you think so? I dropped her off at the front door and drove away."

"Did you see anyone you recognized going in or out of the house?" I asked. "What about Blanche? She was a waiter at the wedding but claims to have left early. Did you see her leaving?"

Hedda paused for a moment, shaking her head before she spoke. "I don't think so, although I don't know if I'd recognize Blanche out of costume."

"You think you might have been the last person Blanche talked to before she was killed as well?"

Hedda's eyes drifted toward the casket. "She came up to me today and told me she wanted to say a few words about Cher." Hedda sighed. "I might not have been gracious to her. I told her a reception celebrating Cher was no place to bring up bad blood or past history."

"Is that what you think she wanted to do?"

"I don't know. She insisted not. She said she wanted to make her peace with Cher. I told her I'd add her to the end of the tributes and we'd get to her if we had time. She wasn't too pleased and stomped off."

I remembered her storming away from me earlier. Blanche had done a lot of stomping off before she was murdered. "Do you have any idea who would want to kill her?"

"You can't help yourself, can you?"

I closed my eyes and did a mental head slap as I recognized the voice behind me. I turned around and tried to give my boyfriend my most innocent smile. "I didn't think this was your district."

Fern stirred against the wall, and Reese looked over at him, shook his head, and looked back at me.

"It's not. Kate called me after she called 911." He cut his eyes to where Kate was flirting with one of the uniforms near the stairs. Richard and Hermes were nowhere to be seen. "I don't know if she understands I don't cover the entire city."

"I don't know if she cares," I said. "I think she considers you our personal detective."

His face finally broke into a half grin. "I don't mind being *your* personal detective." His expression became serious again. "I do mind you trying to do my job. Or actually, the job of the District Three detective."

"I'm sorry." I rested a hand on the sleeve of his brown blazer. "It was an accident. Hedda and I were chatting while we waited for the cops and the questions slipped out."

Reese turned his attention to the brunette in the banana-yellow cocktail dress next to me. "I take it you're Hedda."

"Hedda Lettuce." She dangled a hand in front of his face as she visibly gave him the up-and-down. "You must be the cavalry."

Reese took the hand she clearly meant for him to kiss and gave it a gentle shake back and forth. "I'm a detective with District Two, but since the third district guys are still on their way, I'm here to help secure the scene for them."

I motioned behind me. "Kate and I found the body in the casket when we pulled back the drapes. It's Blanche Davidian, the waiter you were supposed to question about Cher Noble's murder."

Reese sighed. "So this may be my case after all." He stepped around me to get a closer look at the victim, snapping on a pair of latex gloves.

"She couldn't have been killed very long ago, because Kate and I talked to her earlier in the party and so did Hedda," I said.

Reese touched the gold cord around Blanche's neck. "That fits with the general condition of the body. Rigor mortis hasn't even set in."

I looked away quickly and noticed Hedda's eyes were nowhere near the casket either.

"So the casket was empty before the victim was put inside?" Reese asked.

"It was a decorative focal point and was never supposed to have a body inside it." Hedda grimaced. "That would have been gauche."

The Marie Antoinette look-alike in the champagne glass dress crossed in front of us.

"Makes sense," Reese said.

The jazz singer in teal chiffon approached Hedda. "Should the band start playing again, or should we wait for the raffle?"

Reese raised an eyebrow at me but didn't say anything. I knew I would have a lot of explaining to do later.

"Would you like me to make an announcement?" Reese asked Hedda.

Hedda let out a long exhale. "Aren't you a doll? That would be wonderful." She stepped away to talk with the singer, and I pulled Reese over to the tile wall near Fern and away from anyone who could overhear.

"Are you going to tell them there's been a murder?" I whispered, not eager to see a room full of drag queens become more dramatic.

"Yes, but I'm not going to give them any details. They only need to know to stay put until they can give a statement."

"Good. I don't think telling them one of their friends was strangled with a tassel is a good idea."

"I would never tell them something not true," he said, his voice low even though the only person near us was Fern, who was now snoring softly.

I grabbed his sleeve. "What do you mean she wasn't strangled?"

"Oh, she was strangled all right. But not with that cord. It's too thick and the mark around her neck is consistent with the mark around Cher's." He brushed a dark wave of hair off his forehead. "This victim was killed with a wire."

I instinctively raised a hand to my neck. "Garroted?"

Reese's face was grim. "The same MO and probably the same murder weapon means this was almost certainly done by the same killer."

I heard a gasp from below. Fern's eyes were open. "A serial killer?"

CHAPTER 16

I paused on the stone steps leading up to The Line hotel and peered at the massive columns fronting the neoclassical building that had once been a church. I slipped on my sunglasses to shield my eyes from the sun now high in the sky and lifted my face to enjoy the warmth for a moment.

"We owe one to Reese for letting us leave Perry's before anyone else," Kate said as she walked ahead of me toward the tall doors being held open by two uniformed doormen.

"Aside from Richard and Hermes."

"It helped we had an appointment to make and he knows where he can find us." I slid my sunglasses to the top of my head as we entered the hotel lobby. "And I think Richard convinced the cops Hermes was about to piddle on the floor."

To either side of me as we entered the building were staircases leading up, each with a rectangular gold-framed mirror at least twice my height sitting tilted on the floor of the landings. This was on purpose and was considered avant-garde. We continued across the parquet floor, Kate's mules slapping against the wood, and I couldn't help staring at the huge art installation hanging over the expansive high-ceilinged lobby. Made of gold church organ pipes crisscrossing each other and forming a grid, the chandelier looked like a 3D version of the game Pick-Up Sticks. Light streamed in from high windows on all sides of the arched ceiling, and the second-level balcony overlooking the lobby was every bit the choir loft.

Kate stopped and rested her hand on the back of a half-moon blue velvet couch that appeared to seat at least a dozen. "I need coffee. How about you?"

Since the lobby also housed one of the hotel's restaurants, the faint scents of lunch lingered, reminding me it had been hours since I'd eaten. "Definitely. And a croissant if they have one."

"I'll grab it if you want to wait here so we don't miss the client." Kate headed off to the hotel's coffee bar, The Cup We All Race 4, while I crossed to one of the long black tables to the side of the couches. I pulled out a black leather high-backed chair and turned it so I could see the entrance. I did not want to miss our client or Kate's return with caffeine.

As I waited, I thought back to the scene at Perry's. When we'd left, Reese had been assisting the District Three detectives taking statements since there were so many people who'd been in the room when the murder had taken place. I tried to rub away my goosebumps as I remembered talking to Blanche only minutes before she was strangled. It still seemed surreal someone had killed her in a room full of witnesses.

I flashed back to the restaurant and the gold fabric in front of the casket. The hanging velvet had definitely been pulled back when we arrived. Someone, I presumed the killer, must have untied it so they would have cover while they did the deed. The music had been loud enough to drown out any sounds of struggle, and the heavy fabric extended across the entire tiled wall, which meant anyone behind it would not have been seen. I'd told all this to Reese, but I hadn't been able to tell him who had lowered the fabric or slipped behind it. I only hoped one of the other guests had seen something.

My phone buzzed, and I pulled it out of my purse. I shook my head as I read the text message.

"Uh oh," Kate said, walking up to me. "That doesn't look good."

I dropped the phone back into my purse and looked up at her. "Debbie wants us to find an ensemble that can perform the type of music carousels play as they spin around."

"That should drive us all insane within the first hour." She held out a pale-pink ridged paper cup with the words "The Cup We All Race 4" printed on its side and a white wax-paper bag. "Mocha with oat milk and a cinnamon-raisin pastry."

"Oat milk?" I asked.

"It's hip," she told me. "The croissants were whole wheat, so I went another direction."

I took a bite of the sugary swirled pastry and a few flakes fell onto my lap. "Good call."

Kate took a long drink of her coffee. "I still can't get the image of Blanche Davidian out of my head. And Cher Noble."

"I know how you feel." I kept my voice low as a man sat down a few chairs away and opened a laptop. "I can't imagine going the way they did."

Kate made a face. "Not even a feather boa and gold tassel could dress it up."

I agreed with Kate, and from what I'd overheard Reese say to the District Three detectives, I knew he thought the killer's use of the props was meant to make the crimes seem more spontaneous than they were. I wondered if anyone would actually put a hit out on drag queens and why?

I pushed the thought out of my mind. "As awful as it is, we still have weddings to plan." I took another bite of the pastry, the sugar doing its bit to perk me up.

Kate held up her phone. "Speaking of, I got a text from Laurel. She and Mark are running a few minutes behind and will meet us upstairs."

"Let's go." I stood up, taking a sip of the mocha. It was sweet enough so I couldn't tell I was drinking oats. "I'd like to scout out the rooftop without them anyway."

"Promise me you won't start speaking with a British accent when they get here," Kate said as we headed for the back of the hotel and the elevators.

I tried to give her my best scandalized expression as we walked around the reception desk. "I don't know what you're talking about."

Kate sighed. "You know how you are with accents. If someone speaks in one around you for too long, you start to mimic it."

I knew she was right. Our newest groom, Mark, was from London, and after I'd spoken to him on the phone for five minutes, I'd sounded like Eliza Doolittle before her transformation. For this reason, I'd made Kate take the lead on the wedding. Plus, I was prepping her to take weddings on her own so Wedding Belles could expand. I didn't relish the thought of finding someone else to assist me if Kate had her own weddings, but I knew it was time to give her more responsibility.

We stepped into an open elevator and I pressed the button for the roof. "I'll promise if you promise not to look at him like he's a piece of cake."

"Can I help it if he's the best-looking groom we've had in years?" she said, taking a sip of her coffee as we surged up.

"No, but you can keep from drooling. I'm afraid the bride might notice and decide having a wedding planner hot for her groom isn't the best idea."

"You know I would never pursue a groom," Kate said. "It's nice to have one with a full head of hair who's taller than me, though."

"Stefan and Jesse both had hair and were taller than you," I said, reminding her of our recent grooms.

She gave me a side-eye glance. "They don't count. And the groom the week before made me powder the top of his bald head during pictures so it wouldn't create a reflection in the sunlight."

"Why didn't you have Fern do that?" I asked.

"Because Fern has watched too many Kardashian makeup tutorials." She shook her head. "He kept trying to use different shades of powder to contour the guy's head and it was starting to look deformed."

That sounded like Fern.

"It's fine to appreciate our groom," I said as the elevator came to a stop. "Can you do it a little less obviously?"

"I'll try." Kate followed me out of the elevator and almost bumped into me when I stopped abruptly.

"Did you know there would be an event up here?" I asked as a man in black rolled a rack of linens in front of me.

We walked to the open rooftop overlooking the city. The space was bordered by two brick walls covered with crawling vines and fronted with a row of low black planters filled with boxwood. In the distance I could see the Washington Monument, but in front, near the glass railing at the edge of the roof, was a long table draped in white linen with people scurrying around it.

"I don't think it's an event." Kate nudged me and pointed to a photographer setting up a tripod in the corner. "I think it's a styled shoot."

I gave a mental groan. The phenomenon of event planners designing tabletops complete with linens, flowers, china, glassware, menu cards, and even food for the sole purpose of taking pictures of it to splash all over social media was one I'd grown to loathe. I was probably so hostile because Kate and I didn't have the time to create fake events to fill our feeds. We were too busy planning actual weddings (or solving actual crimes).

"Who even does these anymore?" I asked. "You really have to have too much time on your hands."

I watched a woman set a long trough of white flowers in the middle of the table. From her apron, I guessed she was a florist but one I didn't recognize. Then again, floral designers like Buster and Mack, who had plenty of real events, wouldn't be caught dead doing a freebie styled shoot. I recognized a couple of guys from my usual lighting crew on the top of a pair of ladders suspending string lights over the table and a stocky man in a blue suit leaning against one of the brick walls and observing with his arms crossed. Did they hire security for a styled shoot?

"That's Renee," Kate said, waving to a blonde who didn't look much older than her. "I know her from my wedding assistants support group."

I turned to face her. "You have a support group?"

"I didn't mean support group," she said when she saw my face. "It's the drinking group I told you about. It's mostly wedding assistants but also florist assistants and catering assistants. Since we're all twenty-somethings and single, we started hanging out every week or so."

"So whose assistant is Renee?"

Kate tapped her finger to her chin. "I forget. Renee is new to the group. One of Brianna's assistants brought her. Boy, do those girls complain a lot about their boss."

Renee rushed over to us, and I noticed the tips of her hair were dyed pink. She gave Kate an enthusiastic air kiss accompanied by a giggle. "What are you doing here?"

"I was about to ask you the same thing," Kate said, waving at the setup behind her.

Renee giggled again. "It's a styled shoot. We're trying to get in *DC Magazine*." She made a pouty face. "You weren't at Sunday's happy hour."

"We had a rough weekend, so I stayed in." Kate put a hand on my arm. "Renee, this is my boss, Annabelle Archer."

Renee's eyes popped open wide. "I've heard of you."

"Good things, I hope," I said with a laugh, although from the look on Renee's face I wasn't so sure.

"Your White House wedding in *Insider Weddings* magazine was gorgeous," she said, glancing back to Kate and lowering her voice. "But I heard about your wedding on Saturday."

Kate's eyes flicked to me before she answered. "It was pretty upsetting, but we're cooperating with the police to find who did it."

Renee shook her head slowly. "I can't imagine what I would do if our officiant was murdered right before the ceremony."

"It was a first for us," Kate said, her fake laugh falling flat.

"And I heard it was Cher Noble," Renee said. "We almost used her once, but it didn't work out."

"Really?" Now my interest was piqued. "Why not?"

Renee tilted her head while she thought. "I don't remember exactly, but it was a month or so ago. We had to cancel her at the last minute, and I remember she was pretty mad. She called my boss and screamed at her so loudly I could hear it across the room."

I'd never seen Cher Noble angry, but I wouldn't have wanted to cross anyone over six feet tall and three hundred pounds.

"But it was really her fault for not having a cancellation clause in her contract," Renee continued. "We technically didn't owe her a penny. It was not our problem, and that's what my boss told her."

"Who's your boss?" I asked.

"Tina Pink," the bubbly blonde said. "Do you know her?"

Kate and I exchanged a look, and I could tell neither of us was the least bit surprised.

CHAPTER 17

"**R**enee!" The shrill voice was accompanied with a sharp clap of hands. "This is the not the time to socialize."

Tina Pink strode across the open terrace, a pair of sunglasses with the gold Gucci monogram on each side holding her straight blond hair off her face. I noticed she looked too tan for DC in the spring, but the lines around her eyes told me it wasn't courtesy of fake-and-bake or bronzer. I'd bet money she was a tanning bed aficionado.

When she saw me and Kate standing with Renee, she forced a smile. "Oh, it's you two."

"Hi, Tina," Kate returned her fake smile. "Love your white-on-white styled shoot. Cutting-edge."

Tina's expression told me she didn't know if Kate was being sincere or not. "Thanks. Why are you up here?"

"We're showing the space to a client," I answered. "We called ahead to see if the terrace was available a week ago."

Tina twitched one shoulder. "This was last minute. I didn't call the rental order in until last night."

Since their delivery schedules were set the day before, I knew the rental company must have loved that.

"We'll stay out of your way," I said. "Our clients only need a peek at the view and the size of the rooftop."

Renee looked over her shoulder at the table. "Shouldn't the individual cakes be here by now, Tina?"

Tina tapped the sheaf of papers in her hands. "Why don't you read your schedule and tell me, Renee?" She rolled her eyes and gave us a backward look. "I need to get back to work."

Renee followed her as Tina stormed over to the table, saw there were no cakes, and began screaming into her phone at an unnamed baker. I watched as Renee ran toward the elevators and disappeared. If she was smart, she was catching a ride home so she could work on her resignation letter.

"Have I mentioned lately what a great boss you are?" Kate said, her voice low even though Tina couldn't have heard us over her own shrieking.

"She definitely has a temper," I said, observing Tina pacing in front of the long table and waving her arms as she talked.

Kate eyed me. "What are you thinking?"

I gave myself a shake. "Tina is another person who knew Cher, and she happened to have an issue with her."

"But from what Renee said, it sounded like Cher was the wounded party. Not Tina."

I watched Tina's florist cringing under a verbal onslaught regarding the wilted flower Tina shook in the trembling woman's face. "I doubt Tina is ever the wounded party."

Kate focused on something over my shoulder, and her expression changed into one I'd recognize anywhere. There was an attractive man approaching.

"Hi Mark, Laurel," I said as I turned to greet our newest bride and groom.

Laurel was my height with light-brown hair she wore in a pixie cut, and Mark had wavy, dark hair and starkly contrasting blue eyes. I thought our bride was adorable and our groom swoon worthy. I pinched Kate's leg to remind her to behave.

"This view is pretty great," Laurel said as she leaned in to give me a quick hug before giving one to Kate.

"If the weather is good, it's amazing," I agreed, hugging the groom and ensuring Kate let him go when it was her turn.

"I love the brick walls," Mark said.

"Aren't they smashing?" I said.

Kate shot me a look and mouthed the word "smashing?" to me as the bride and groom admired the cityscape. I gave myself a mental head slap. Had I said it in my version of a British accent? I hoped not.

"Did you do this for us?" Laurel asked, taking a few steps toward the long white table.

"I'm afraid not," Kate walked with her. "Another planner is doing a styled shoot."

"It's pretty," the bride said, twisting around to catch her fiancé's eye, "but a little plain for us, right?"

"Right, love," he said. "We like color."

I smiled, afraid to speak for fear a Cockney accent would come bursting out of my mouth. A breeze blew across the terrace, kicking up the table linen and making me rub my bare forearms.

Renee appeared from the direction of the elevator rolling a gray cart topped with small white cakes adorned with white sugar flowers. Tina stalked over to her, and the two of them began setting the cakes at each place setting. As I took in the white linen, white flowers, white plates, and white cakes, I felt like yawning. If this was Tina's idea of an earth-shattering design, I didn't know how long she'd make it in the wedding world.

Kate put a hand on the bride's arm. "There's a lot more you can do with this space. We could hang paper lanterns or project light patterns onto the brick walls."

"This is only one of many looks T Pink can design for you." Tina turned from her table and pressed a business card into the bride's hand. "If you haven't already booked a planner, I'd be happy to meet with you and tell you why I would be a better choice."

Kate's mouth fell open, and Laurel flicked her gaze to the business card covered in bright-pink swirls. Kate snatched the card from the bride's open palm and tucked it into her pocket. "You won't be needing that."

"We're happy with Wedding Belles," Laurel stammered. "But thanks."

Tina laughed. "You can't blame a girl for trying."

Watch me, I thought.

"She's not one of yours, is she?" the groom asked me, clearly confused by what had happened.

"Not by a long shot," I said.

Renee wheeled the empty cart past me, her cheeks red and her eyes down. Tina followed her and looked like she was about to launch into a tirade when she spotted me standing with the groom. To be clear, when she spotted the groom. Even from a few feet away I could see her pupils dilate and her mouth widen into a predatory smile.

"Are you the . . .?" Tina let the question dangle as she looked back at his fiancé and raised an eyebrow, making it clear she found the pairing hard to believe.

Mark crossed his arms over his chest. "I think the word you may be searching for is fiancé."

"Of course," Tina giggled as she moved closer. "I thought maybe you were the brother or best friend. Hoped, I guess."

Did this woman have no shame? I angled myself in front of the groom so she couldn't get any closer. "Did I hear the rumors correctly? You recently got married, Tina?"

Her smile flickered. "That's right." She flashed an admittedly huge diamond. "Almost a year."

"How's life as a newlywed?"

She pulled her eyes off the groom to answer me. "Great. We

moved into a new house. It's way too big for the two of us, but with my husband's high profile, we can't live in any old place."

"What does your husband do?" I asked. The age-old question everyone asked in Washington.

"He owns a bunch of nightclubs downtown." Tina tossed her hair off her shoulder. "Everyone in DC knows him. He's around here somewhere actually." She made an exaggerated frowny face. "You're still single, right?"

"Yep." I tried to catch Kate's eye so she could join us. We really needed to come up with a nonverbal emergency signal.

"It must be sad planning weddings for the rest of the world and never having one of your own." Tina smiled while she said it, but the words were sharp.

The groom's eyes darted between Tina and me. I told myself not to let her words bother me, although the truth of them stung, and I felt my throat tighten.

"Is that how you met your husband? Nightclubs?" I asked, trying to keep my voice from cracking.

She tilted her head at me. "Did you hear that through the grapevine too?"

"An educated guess," I said, dropping my eyes to her short skirt and seeing her press her lips together in response. It was easy to see Tina as a club hopper. I'd never seen her in an outfit that wouldn't be at home with techno music and strobe lights.

Mark took his fianceé's hand as she and Kate joined us. "Ready to go, love?"

I didn't give Tina another look as we headed toward the elevator bank, but I spotted Renee still standing with the cart.

"I'm really sorry," she said, stepping close to Kate and me and keeping her voice low so Tina couldn't hear. "I saw she tried to steal your client."

Kate put an arm around her shoulder. "It's not your fault."

"And we would never leave Annabelle and Kate," Laurel said.

"No other planner can do a British accent even half as well as Annabelle," Mark said, giving me a wink.

I felt my cheeks flush. "You've noticed?"

The groom gave me a playful nudge. "I think it's smashing."

Kate let out a breath. "I'm so glad this is out in the open. I've been trying to get her to stop since you hired us, but she doesn't even know she's doing it."

The elevator opened. Mark and Laurel looked at us and the oversized cart. We wouldn't all fit inside.

"You two go ahead," I said. "We'll take the next one."

They agreed and promised to call us later with a final decision on the rooftop. Laurel blew us kisses as the doors closed.

Kate turned to face Renee. "Plus, we aren't foolish enough to bring a client around without having a signed contract."

"Really?" Renee shook her head. "Tina takes clients to site visits all the time before they sign with us. They don't always end up going with her and she goes berserk."

"I wouldn't want to have to deal with her temper." I cast a glance behind me, but Tina had gone back to her table and was loudly micromanaging the photographer.

"It's awful," Renee said. "She's bad on-site, but she's even worse in the office where no one but me or the other girls can see. I'm thinking of going back to waiting tables."

"Come on." Kate squeezed her shoulder. "Not all planners are like that. You need to quit working for her and start working for someone else."

Renee bit her bottom lip. "I'm afraid to leave her. She might get as mad at me as she gets at other people. I don't want anyone to say about me what she's said about Melody or Cher or the barista who messed up her lactose-free latte."

The elevator arrived and the doors opened with a bing. Kate stepped inside and held the door open.

"Wait a second." I helped Renee push the cart inside the

elevator car. "Did you say Cher? Why was she mad at Cher? I thought Cher was the one angry at her."

"At first," Renee said. "Then Tina heard Cher had been telling people she was disorganized and canceled things at the last minute. She hit the roof. I don't think I've ever heard her so angry."

"So she hated Cher as much as Cher hated her?" Kate asked.

"I'd say so," Renee said. "Tina told me she wished that Vegas wannabe would drop dead."

CHAPTER 18

"I'm glad you could get away long enough for dinner," I said to Reese as a waiter directed us to a table for two by the wall of windows overlooking the Georgetown street. Headlights flashed in the darkness as cars passed, but the sounds of the horns were muffled.

Reese pulled out my chair for me. "I was ready for a break after most of the day spent processing the new crime scene."

I stammered a thank you and hoped I wasn't blushing and people weren't staring. Most guys in DC did not pull out chairs or open doors anymore—something Richard considered a modern-day tragedy and a symptom of the downfall of humanity. Part of me wished Richard could see this, but another part of me was afraid he might actually be somewhere in the restaurant spying on me.

I unfolded the black napkin onto my lap, pleased it wasn't white and I wouldn't have tiny fibers all over my black dress at the end of the meal. "Have you been at Perry's this entire time?"

Reese slid off his brown blazer and hung it off the back of his chair, revealing a blue button-down showing off his broad chest.

"I left before the District Three guys did, but it still took a long time to talk to all the guests."

Our waiter appeared, dropping a basket of two large salty pretzels on the table, and we placed our order—the crab cake sandwich and a glass of white wine for me and a blue cheese burger and a pale ale for him.

"You're not a salad girl." Reese leaned back in his chair. "I like that."

I swallowed a mouthful of soft pretzel. "That bodes well for us because I almost never eat salad. It gives Richard fits. He's convinced I'm going to die of malnutrition."

Reese winked at me. "A good reason not to eat it if it gives Richard something to fuss about."

I smiled at him, trying to keep my eyes from drifting down to his muscled chest and shoulders. "Exactly." I noticed his hazel eyes deepen to green and cleared my throat. "So did you learn anything good at the scene today?"

He leaned his elbows on the edge of the table and steepled his fingers. "I'm not supposed to talk to you about an open investigation, Annabelle."

"I know." I took another bite of the soft pretzel, enjoying the salty kick. "I thought we could do a little quid pro quo."

Reese raised an eyebrow. "How would that work since you're not supposed to be involved in the case anymore? Did you have another kind of trade in mind?"

Kate would have jumped at the idea of another type of trade and possibly abandoned the idea of dinner altogether. I shook my head. "Not exactly. I happened upon some information today."

Reese exhaled slowly. "How does that even happen? You're a wedding planner. Most people in your line of work never get involved in a single murder investigation their entire careers. But you . . ."

"You know I don't go looking for trouble." I took a sip of the cold white wine the waiter placed in front of me.

GROOMED FOR MURDER

"Do I?" he asked. "I have met your friends, remember?"

I held up one palm. "You can't hold Leatrice against me. It's not my fault I moved into a building with a one-woman neighborhood watch."

"At least she's more Inspector Clouseau than Sherlock Holmes, otherwise the department would be in real trouble."

I decided not to remind him of the time Leatrice, along with some questionable friends she picked up from the dark net, had hacked into the DC police department computers and fed me information about a case. Better not to open old wounds or remind Reese of the many times I'd gone against his strict orders to stay away from an investigation.

Reese took a drink of his amber-colored beer. "So what information did you stumble upon today while out planning weddings?"

I decided to let his slightly sarcastic tone slide.

"Have you heard me mention a new planner called Tina Pink?" I asked as our waiter placed my crab cake sandwich and fries in front of me. I dipped one of my thick-cut fries in the ramekin of tartar sauce.

Reese glanced up from assembling his burger. "I don't think so."

I waved a hand. "It doesn't matter. I only met her on Sunday. Anyway, she already has a reputation for leaving her old boss in a pretty sleazy way, and she's become BFFs with another awful planner who trashes everyone in the business."

Reese nodded as he chewed, so I continued. "Kate and I were showing one of our couples a venue this afternoon, and who do you think we ran into on the rooftop of The Line hotel? Tina Pink doing a sad white-on-white styled shoot."

"Does this story somehow connect to the murders?" Reese asked.

I finished the fry and took a bite of my pickle spear. "I thought you had to be patient to be a detective."

He put down his burger. "Babe, I spent the day talking to a room full of drag queens. I honestly don't know how much patience I have left in me."

Fair enough, I thought. "Long story short, Tina Pink's assistant told us she'd gotten in a big blowout fight with Cher Noble."

"Interesting," Reese said. "Was the fight serious enough to kill over?"

"Tina has a pretty bad temper. Plus, her assistant said she heard Tina saying she wanted to kill Cher for telling people she was a bad planner."

Reese took a swig of his beer. "How big is this Tina woman?"

"A little taller than me, a little skinnier, and a lot blonder. A total salad girl."

Reese grinned. "As much as she may have wanted to kill Cher, there's no way a woman that size could overpower a man who was over six feet tall and north of three hundred pounds. And unless she was wearing a great disguise, she wasn't on the security footage from Meridian House."

"You watched the footage?"

He ran a finger around the top of his beer glass. "It wasn't too helpful. No shots of the murder scene, lots of setup people walking around in baseball caps, so few face shots, but no tall blonde."

I thought about it for a second as I took a bite of my crab cake sandwich. Reese was right. Not only was Tina not strong enough, I doubted she would risk breaking a nail to kill someone as violently as Cher was murdered. And, as far as I knew, she had no connection to Blanche Davidian.

"Can you confirm the two murders were connected?" I asked Reese.

"I'm not officially telling you one way or the other." Reese dropped his voice. "But the MO is exactly the same, including being garroted by a wire and wrapping another object around the neck unconnected to the strangling. Not even a copycat killer would know since we've been careful about keeping it out of the press."

I shivered a little even though the restaurant wasn't cool. I hated thinking about the way in which Cher and Blanche were killed, and I couldn't imagine hating someone so much. "So whoever did the first murder did the second one."

"Drat," I said, picking up a fry and tossing it back onto the plate. "I really wanted Tina to be the killer, but not only was she not at the scene of the first murder, she wasn't at Perry's this morning either."

"So you're trying to convince yourself this Tina is the killer even though she wasn't at either crime scene?" Reese gave a low whistle. "You really don't like this planner, do you?"

"She actually tried to steal our clients from us today while I was standing right in front of her." I wrinkled my nose. "She's the worst kind of wedding planner—unpleasant, unorganized, unethical."

"Sounds like she's the anti-Annabelle."

I smiled. I liked the sound of that. "Absolutely. Like the opposite of a mini-me."

Reese reached his hand across the table and placed it on top of mine. "I've had to deal with some pretty bad apples in my work too. All I can tell you is the cream rises to the top. You keep doing the great work you always do, and you and Kate won't have to worry. No matter how many new planners pop up."

I looked down and blinked hard so I wouldn't cry. That might have been the nicest thing a guy had ever said to me regardless of the mixed metaphors. I squeezed his hand. "Thanks."

He squeezed back. "I'm glad your big clue wasn't a real lead. I've got so many things to follow up on after questioning everyone from this morning, I don't know if I could have handled one more."

"Did anyone see anything suspicious?" I asked. "Someone had to have seen who lowered those drapes, right? I can't think of any reason to lower them unless you needed to do something you wanted to be sure no one saw. Like strangle someone."

"I really shouldn't tell you this considering your connection." Reese looked down at his lap.

"Tell me what? What connection?" I asked. "You mean because I was at both crime scenes?"

Reese gave an abrupt shake of his head. "Two people mentioned seeing someone near the gold velvet or messing with the fabric."

"Did they recognize the person or give a description? Almost everyone at the reception had on a pretty distinctive outfit."

"Neither of them remembers a face. They only saw a glimpse of the person from the back, so they could only give me one defining characteristic. But they both said the same thing, so that's a sign we're on the right track."

I leaned over the table. "What was it?"

"The person they saw—a man—wore all black. Possibly a black suit."

I straightened up. "A black suit? Most guests were in a crazy cocktail dress. The only person I noticed in a black suit was . . . " I covered my mouth with my hand.

"Fern," Reese said for me.

"Can I tempt you two with dessert?" the waiter asked as he cleared our empty pretzel basket. "Our chocolate lava cake is to die for."

Reese and I both shook our heads.

CHAPTER 19

"What do you mean he dropped you off with a good-night kiss?" Kate asked the next morning when I opened my apartment door still wearing my grungiest pajamas. She eyed the worn plaid drawstring bottoms. "I mean, I'm relieved you didn't have him sleep over and wear those hideous things, but I don't understand why he left."

"It kind of ruined the mood to discover he has to bring in one of my best friends for questioning about Blanche's murder."

Kate pressed a hand to her throat and tightened her grip on the white paper bakery bag in her other hand.

"Not you," I said as I watched her visibly relax. "It's Fern."

Kate dropped her pink purse to the floor and sank onto the couch, her green silk shorts leaving lots of exposed leg for her to tuck under her. "I thought we already went through this with the questioning at the station and the makeovers."

"About Cher's murder." I padded barefoot into my kitchen, talking through the open space between the two rooms divided by a waist-high counter and retractable wooden shutters I never closed. I opened the refrigerator and pulled out two bottled

Mocha Frappuccinos. I shook them as I walked back to the living room. "This is about Blanche's murder."

"The police think Fern had something to do with Blanche Davidian being murdered?" Kate took the bottled coffee I extended to her and handed me the white bakery bag. "Did Fern even know Blanche?"

I twisted the top off my drink and sat down next to Kate on the couch, peering into the bag and being hit with the scent of sugar. "Not that I know of, but Fern is always full of surprises. For all we know, he styled Blanche's wigs as well."

"Can you hand me the one with chocolate icing?"

I passed her the oversized vanilla cupcake wrapped in wax paper and topped with chocolate buttercream. "Cupcakes for breakfast?"

Kate dipped one finger into the icing. "I figured you'd either need the calorie replacement or the comfort of sugar. I got you the Razmanian Devil since I know you like raspberry and lemon."

I pulled the familiar lemon cupcake crowned with lemon icing and a tiny red fondant heart out of the bag. I took a bite, knowing the raspberry filling was in the center. The rush of sweet and tart made me close my eyes and smile. "Good call."

"So the police are interested in talking to Fern because he may have styled the victim's wigs?" Kate asked, peeling the wax paper away from her cupcake so she could take a bigger bite.

"I wish that was it. Apparently, two witnesses at Perry's claim to have seen a man in all black pulling the gold velvet down in front of the casket. Can you remember anyone else at the reception wearing a black suit?"

Kate took a swig of her coffee. "I don't remember anyone there who wasn't in sequins except maybe Jesse. He was in a navy suit, wasn't he?"

"That's right. Was Stefan wearing something dark too?" I tried to remember his outfit from the brief glimpse I'd gotten of him heading toward the stairs, but I drew a blank. The only thing I could say for sure was he wasn't in sequins.

"I didn't see him, but doesn't he always wear black?" Kate said. "I do know there's no way Jesse could have killed Blanche. We were talking to him right before we found Fern and went up to the stage. Plus, he's not the type."

I agreed with Kate. Jesse didn't have opportunity or motive. I couldn't imagine why either groom would want to kill Blanche. As far as I knew, they'd never laid eyes on her.

"So it couldn't have been Jesse and we don't know about Stefan," I said.

"If the same person killed both drag queens, it couldn't have been Stefan. We know he didn't kill Cher. He was more upset than anyone," Kate said. "It almost ruined his wedding, and we both know how obsessed he was with having the perfect wedding."

"There must have been someone else because it wasn't Jesse or Stefan, and you and I both know Fern could never kill anyone."

Kate dropped her crumpled-up wax paper in the empty bakery bag. "At least he could never strangle anyone. I wouldn't put it past him to slowly poison someone for wearing a mullet or having frosted tips."

"If we follow that logic, Richard would knock off every person who dared to put ketchup on his filet mignon."

"I'm surprised he hasn't," Kate said.

Come to think of it, so was I. I finished my cupcake and coffee as I thought about how dramatic my friends were and how dramatic the wedding industry was in general. I bet paralegals didn't have these types of work problems.

"Does Fern have any idea he's a suspect in Blanche's murder?" Kate asked, taking the paper bag and both of our empty bottles and heading for the kitchen.

"Promise you won't breathe a word to Reese?" I called out as I heard her open my foot-pedal-operated trash can.

"Cross my heart," she said as the trash can lid clanged shut.

"I may have left a message on Fern's voicemail giving him a heads-up."

Kate's head popped up over the kitchen divider. "I'm guessing you weren't supposed to?"

I shook my head. "Reese wasn't even supposed to tell me."

Kate made a clucking noise with her tongue as she came back into the living room. "I guess you don't need to worry about the kind of PJs you wear after all."

"You really think he'll be angry enough to break up with me?" I asked, my stomach fluttering.

"Reese?" Kate gave me a knowing look. "How do you think he'll react when he finds out you actually tipped off his only suspect? What do you think his superior will think?"

I bit the edge of my fingernail. "I guess I didn't think it through, but I didn't want Fern to be ambushed by the police and have a nervous breakdown."

"Don't get me wrong. I would have done exactly the same thing. But I'm not dating the hot detective. Have I mentioned the cute sous chef I met the other night?"

"I thought you were dating a guy who works at the State Department."

Kate wrinkled her nose. "I'm off politics, but I did meet a nice reporter from *Politico*. I'm thinking of having dinner with him."

"Not at the restaurant where the other guy is a sous chef, I hope."

Kate looked scandalized. "Of course not. I'm not an amateur, you know."

I did know. Considering the number of men Kate dated and juggled successfully, I would never call her an amateur. My mind wandered back to my love life.

"Maybe Reese won't have to find out. I can call Fern and tell him I was mistaken." I snapped my fingers. "Better yet, I can offer to arrange a meeting with Reese and Fern. I'll act as the liaison."

Kate pulled her phone out of her purse and looked at the screen. "Well, you'll have to do that later, because we have to pick up Alexandra from the airport in less than an hour."

I groaned. In my preoccupation with Fern being a potential murder suspect, I'd completely forgotten the cake baker for Debbie and Darla's baby shower cake was flying in this morning.

Alexandra had been our go-to cake designer for years before she'd up and moved to Scotland. She'd claimed it was for the highland scenery and men in kilts, but I knew it had been the only way she could escape the crazy Type-A Washington brides. The more in demand her elaborate and delicious cakes had become, the more exacting and impossible her clients had grown. At the time, I'd thought her moving to another continent had been extreme. Now, I wasn't so sure.

Because she loved us and because we promised she never had to speak to or lay eyes on the clients, Alexandra agreed to fly back for our most important cakes. Since she'd done the cake for Debbie's wedding, there was never a question she'd do the baby shower cake. Plus, we loved the excuse to see her.

"Give me ten minutes to throw on clothes," I said as I hurried down the hallway to my bedroom. "In the meantime, can you call Fern? Calm him down, make up something comforting, tell him we'll be over later?"

"You got it."

It took me less than ten minutes to pull on jeans and a pale-blue button-down and put on enough makeup so Kate wouldn't complain I was going for an Amish chic look.

"Bad news," Kate said when I reappeared in the living room. "Fern's not answering. I tried his cell three times, and I called the salon. No dice."

I tried to ignore the growing knot in my stomach. "Maybe he's sleeping in."

Kate raised her eyebrows but didn't respond. We both knew Fern was an early riser.

I grabbed my black purse from where I usually left it on the floor beside the couch and felt it vibrating. I dug my phone out and checked the display. "Reese," I whispered to Kate as if he could hear me.

"Answer it," she said. "It could be nothing."

"And if it's not?"

She blinked at me as I pressed the talk button.

"Hey!" I tried to make my voice sound as cheery and normal as possible as I followed Kate out of my apartment and locked the door behind us. "What's up?"

"I've tried your friend Fern at his home and work and he isn't there." He paused. "He wouldn't happen to be at your place, would he?"

I sighed, grateful to be able to give him an honest answer. "Nope. I haven't seen or talked to Fern since Perry's yesterday."

Kate began to walk down the stairs, her heels slapping against the floor. I followed her, my black ballet flats almost stealthy in comparison.

"Any idea where he might be?" Reese asked.

"Not really." Again, another honest answer.

"Okay. I'll talk to you later, babe."

"Bye." I could tell he was exasperated, and I was glad it wasn't with me. Yet.

When we reached the ground level, I stopped and jerked my head toward the apartment door closest to the building entrance. "I need to tell Leatrice about the shipment we might be getting for the shower. I do not want it returned, so I need her to keep an eye out for the UPS guy."

"Easy. Doesn't she love the UPS guy?"

I knocked on Leatrice's door. "She only recently gave up on me marrying him."

The wooden door opened a crack and Leatrice's eye appeared. "Hello, dear. What can I do for you?"

It was unusual for my overly involved neighbor not to come bounding out of her apartment with a thousand questions about where I was going and an equal number of reasons why she should come along. "Is everything okay?"

"Fine and dandy," she said, not widening the opening in the door as I tried to look over her head into the apartment.

"What's on your head?" Kate asked, drawing my attention to her yellow towel turban.

Leatrice's cheeks colored as she touched a hand to her head. "I decided to change my hair color, that's all."

My suspicion was piqued. The only time I'd known Leatrice to change her hair color was when it was done for her. By Fern.

"Is Fern with you?" I asked.

"No." She shook her head, but her contorted facial expression told me she was lying. "It's just me."

I heard a muffled voice from inside the apartment and her head jerked inside before reappearing.

"And Perry Mason. Another marathon."

"Perry Mason does not sound that prissy," I said, pushing the door open with one hand to reveal Fern at Leatrice's dining room table wearing a matching yellow towel on his head. I could see bottles of developer, tubes of color, various combs, mixing bowls, and measuring cups spread in front of him.

"Who are you calling prissy?" he asked, adjusting his floral print smock over his shoulders.

"Why are you here and not at work?" Kate asked. "Please tell me you're not getting matching perms or something."

"Now that's an idea," Leatrice said. "They'd never recognize us with big curls."

"What are you talking about?" I looked from Leatrice to Fern.

Leatrice bounced up and down on her toes. "We're changing our appearance so we can go on the lam."

"I got your message. I refuse to go to prison, Annabelle." Fern stood, his smock swirling around him as he spun to face me. "I'm making a run for it."

"And I'm driving," Leatrice said.

Reese was going to kill me.

CHAPTER 20

"I 'm afraid to ask what color you're dyeing your hair," I said to Leatrice as I stepped inside her apartment and let my eyes adjust to the lower light.

Leatrice didn't get as much natural light on the first floor as I did on the fourth, and she kept her blinds closed for fear of being spied on. Since her apartment was on the same side of the building as mine, her layout was similar. But where mine was minimalist and lacking in any decorative items not connected to a wedding, hers was filled with bright patterns and plenty of knickknacks.

She patted her towel turban. "Since I've been a blonde for a while, Fern thought it would confuse the fuzz if I went back to brunette. Make it easier for us to disappear."

"The fuzz?" I put a hand over my nose to block some of the ammonia smell and said a little prayer of thanks Fern hadn't decided to color her hair pink or blue.

"And are you going blond?" Kate asked Fern.

Fern sucked in his breath. "Heavens, no. I only added a few burnished-copper highlights for the spring."

"That should confuse the police," Kate muttered to me.

"All of this because the police want to talk to you about Blanche's murder?" I dropped my purse onto Leatrice's floral print couch since her coffee table was covered with paperback mystery novels.

"They're trying to frame me." Fern's eyes welled up with tears. "I didn't even know Blanche very well, and I certainly didn't have any reason to kill her, so how am I a person of interest?"

Leatrice hurried over and put a spindly arm around his shoulder. "We think it's a setup."

"Why would the police want to set up Fern?" I asked, feeling my eye twitch coming on. "I know Reese wouldn't. He really likes you."

That may have been an overstatement of Reese's feelings about Fern, but I knew he didn't have a problem with him.

Fern pulled down the corner of the yellow towel wrapped around his head and dabbed his eyes. "Well, isn't he a sweetheart? I've always liked him too. And for what it's worth, I don't agree with Richard."

Knowing how jealous Richard was of Reese, I didn't dare ask for clarification.

"Fern and I think the real killer is setting him up," Leatrice said. "It's all an elaborate hoax."

"How?" I asked. "By tricking Fern into wearing a black suit to the reception for Cher?"

Leatrice pursed her bright-coral lips. "We haven't worked out all the details yet."

Fern sat up in his chair. "What's this about my suit?"

"That's why they want to talk to you," Kate said, walking over to the table and examining the tubes of hair color. "Two witnesses mentioned seeing a man in all black fiddling with the gold fabric in front of the casket. Since the killer clearly lowered it so no one could see him strangle Blanche, they think it might have been the same person."

"But it couldn't have been me," Fern said. "I was helping one of the girls with her hair right up until about two minutes before I saw you two and introduced you to Hedda Lettuce."

Leatrice clapped her hands. "An alibi!"

"Can the woman back you up?"

"Pat Dry?" Fern said. "Of course she can. Her wig was all catty-cornered, and I evened it up for her."

"Her drag name is Pat Dry?" Kate asked.

Fern touched a hand to his turban. "She was in a pale-pink number with lots of bugle beads."

"Perfect," I said. "All we need to do is tell your story to Detective Reese and let him follow up with Ms. Dry to confirm it."

"I feel like the weight of the world is off my shoulders." Fern stood up and began packing his supplies inside a nylon bag.

"Wait a second," Kate said. "That still leaves some guy in all black who messed with the velvet fabric and probably killed Blanche. Shouldn't we be worried?"

Fern flinched. "I can't stand the thought of someone being strangled a few feet away from where the rest of us were drinking it up. It's horrible we didn't see or hear a thing."

"Someone had to see or hear something." Leatrice went over to a tall wooden bookcase and pulled out a thick paperback volume. "According to *The Everything Private Investigation Book*, witnesses can be notoriously unreliable and forgetful. I'm sure some of the guests saw things they don't know are clues."

Looking at the book's dog-eared pages, I wondered how many times Leatrice had referred to the manual when surveiling our neighbors or questioning the postman on his whereabouts when he was late with the mail.

"Where were you when you were fixing Pat Dry's hair?" Kate asked Fern.

Fern bent over at the waist and shook out his hair. "Close to the band. She was one of the singers getting ready to go on after the tributes. I couldn't have her performing with Leaning Tower of Pisa hair, now could I?"

Kate grabbed my arm. "I thought I saw Fern near us at some point, because I saw the back of a dark suit, but it couldn't have been him if he was near the band. So some other man was there in a black suit."

I thought back to the reception at Perry's and remembered talking to Blanche for a while and listening to the singers before finding Fern again and meeting Hedda Lettuce. I did remember seeing a glimpse of someone in black who wasn't Fern or our grooms, and I recalled noticing the fabric was down at some point. I rubbed my temples. It was all so muddled, and I couldn't remember any details about the other man in black.

"You're right," I said. "There was someone else in black aside from us, Fern, and Jesse. I'm going to call Reese and tell him what we know."

I pulled my phone out of my purse and dialed Reese's number from my list of recent calls as Fern began combing out Leatrice's once-again jet-black hair. Since I'd known her, Leatrice had gone from Wayne Newton black to electric burgundy to platinum blonde. I had no idea her real hair color or what it had been when she was younger, although I suspected it was heavily gray underneath the dye. It was hard to imagine Leatrice anything but the eighty-year-old I knew her to be.

"Hey, babe," Reese said. "Is everything okay?"

I realized we'd spoken less than half an hour ago, and we normally weren't the kind of couple to talk throughout the day. I took a few steps toward the shelving unit holding Leatrice's turntable and her collection of vinyl records.

"I have good news. I found Fern and he has an alibi."

"Okay," he said slowly. "Where is he?"

"He's with Leatrice." I flipped through the record covers, their paper edges soft from age and being handled. "They're finishing up their hair."

"Should I ask?"

"Probably not." I picked out a big band album and looked at

the tuxedoed men on the front, smiling as they held their instruments. "But I also wanted to tell you Kate and I remember another man in black at Perry's. We can't remember anything about him, but we know there was someone else at the party in black other than Fern and our grooms."

Reese sighed on the other end. "Not too helpful. And what do you mean 'our grooms?'"

"Our grooms from Saturday, Jesse and Stefan, were at Perry's yesterday. They hadn't left for their honeymoon, so they came to pay their respects."

"Well, I didn't interview them."

"Maybe they left before you arrived. I did see them near the stairs before Richard secured the scene."

"I should talk to them. When are they leaving for their honeymoon?"

"Next week." I tapped my fingers on the album cover. "Wait a second. There were way more people in black. I totally forgot about the band. Those guys were in tuxes."

"Weren't they playing the whole time?"

"Bands always take breaks and sometimes one member at a time takes a break while the others play, especially in jazz groups. One of the band guys could have snuck away for a couple of minutes."

"Good information. We questioned the band but didn't ask if they'd taken breaks or switched out."

I replaced the album. "Happy to help, Detective."

He laughed quietly. "I like it when you call me Detective. It reminds me of when I first met you and you and your crew were always trying to give me the runaround."

"What?" I tried to sound shocked. "Us?"

"Nice try, but completely unbelievable. I'll check out the band, but can you ask Fern to swing by the station to make a statement about his alibi so we can clear him?" He paused, and I wondered if he was flashing back to the last time Fern had been in the precinct, and he'd almost turned it into a beauty salon. "On second thought, I'll come to him. Where will he be?"

"Reese wants to come take your statement," I said to Fern as I held my hand over the phone's speaker. "Where will you be?"

Fern paused and glanced down at Leatrice's wet hair. "Right here until I get her set and blown dry."

"Leatrice's apartment," I told Reese.

"Will I get to see you?" he asked, his voice low, and I heard chattering in the background.

I took a peek at my phone's clock. "Nope. Kate and I are late to pick up our cake designer."

Kate looked at her own phone and yelped. She grabbed my phone and headed for the door. "She'll call you later, lover boy. We've got to fly." She clicked off the phone and tossed it back to me.

"Seriously?" I ran after her, out Leatrice's door and the entrance to the building. Luckily, my car was parked out front and we both jumped in.

Kate threw on her seatbelt while I started the engine. "Churn rubber, Annabelle!"

CHAPTER 21

"Were you waiting long?" I asked as Alexandra lowered the square cake box into my back seat.

The willowy baker tossed her long chestnut hair over her shoulder and smiled, sitting down next to me and pulling the hem of her striped maxi dress into the car before closing the door. "I'd barely walked out of the terminal when you pulled up."

Seeing Alexandra again reminded me how little she looked like what you'd imagine of a baker. Instead of being round and jolly, she was thin and elegant. Her clothes were chic and never covered in flour, and she spoke with a slight European accent she breezily explained as "a little bit of everywhere." When she'd lived in DC, she'd been a media darling since she was as photogenic as her cakes, and her upbeat charm had made it easy for us to sell her. I was glad she was back, even if it was only for a few days.

Kate had moved to the back seat so Alexandra could sit in the front, and she patted the top of the white cardboard box. "Did you fly the cake over from Scotland in your lap?"

Alexandra laughed. "No. These are the gum paste carousel

horses I made ahead. They're wrapped in tissue paper so they won't break, but I still didn't want to check them with the airline."

Even from the front seat I could smell the sugar of the gum paste. Alexandra was famous for her sugar flowers and the loose sugar petals she scattered around her cakes. I'd eaten many an edible petal at the end of weddings and could attest to the rush of energy a handful of them could produce. Even smelling the concentrated sugar perked me up.

"Do you want to go to your hotel or your rented studio space?" I asked, as the airport security officer waved at me to move out of the loading and unloading lane. I waved back and checked my blind spot before edging out into the slow-moving traffic and merging into the stream of cars headed back into the city.

"Would you mind terribly if we swung by Lush?" Alexandra asked. "Buster and Mack want to show me the floral palette they picked so I can match the fondant perfectly."

"You got it." I took the exit for the Key Bridge and we crossed over the Potomac River.

"So how are the plans for the shower coming along?" Alexandra asked, looking across the dark-blue river as a brave crew team skimmed across the surface of the still-frigid water.

Kate leaned her head between the two front seats. "We haven't had much time to think about the shower. We're still cleaning up after our wedding on Saturday."

Alexandra twisted to face Kate. "Which one was that?"

"Two grooms. Big budget. High profile."

"Who did the cake?" Alexandra asked. Always her first question about any wedding.

"No cake," I said, making a right onto M Street and entering the Georgetown shopping district. "We did a stack of cheese wheels."

"The grooms avoid sugar," Kate explained. "But they love really good cheese."

Alexandra made a face like she didn't approve of this decision. "What about their guests? Didn't some of them want cake?"

"I'm sure they did, but the wedding wasn't really about the guests," I said.

"It was about Stefan," Kate said. "Until it was about Cher Noble."

Alexandra held up a finger. "I beg your pardon?"

Kate giggled. "I keep forgetting how odd that sounds. She was our drag queen officiant who got strangled before the ceremony."

That didn't sound any less odd.

Alexandra gasped and put a hand to her own neck. "How awful." She shook her head slowly. "And another murder at one of your weddings. Rotten luck, ladies."

"Tell us about it." I paused at a red light and glanced at the restaurant where Reese and I had eaten the night before. The windows were open and a few guests had already staked out their lunch tables with a view of the sidewalk. I looked away, hoping future dates would end better.

"Who would want to kill the wedding officiant before the wedding?" Alexandra asked.

"Someone who really wanted her dead, because it was not a pretty sight," Kate said.

Alexandra's mouth fell open. "You found the body too? I'm starting to think this isn't bad luck. Are you sure someone isn't trying to ruin your business?"

I exchanged a look with Kate in the rearview mirror. "There are a few planners we don't like, but I can't imagine them committing murder so they can take our weddings. Not even Brianna."

"And a second drag queen was murdered yesterday, so it looks more like someone has it out for drag queens than for us," Kate said.

I turned down a side street and found a parking spot a few doors down from Buster and Mack's storefront, parallel parking my car quickly while a car behind me waited. Alexandra and Kate stepped out, and I followed them down the block and into the glass-fronted flower shop topped with a pale-green awning.

As we stepped inside the shop and a bell tinkled overhead to announce our arrival, I inhaled the aroma of fresh flowers. Rows of open white roses, fluffy pink peonies, and golden ranunculus sat in galvanized metal buckets on chrome racks along one wall. The rest of the open space was taken up by a long metal table surrounded by matching barstools and a tricked-out cappuccino station behind it. The concrete floors combined with all the metal to give the flower shop a hip, industrial look. Just like its owners.

"Thank heavens you're here." Mack hurried toward us with the chains on his black leather outfit echoing off the metal and glass. He gave us all air kisses and Alexandra an extra hug. "Buster is on a tear."

"What about?" I asked, hearing the larger man storming around in the back of the shop.

Mack bit the edge of one thumbnail. "Have you heard of a new planner called Tina Pink?"

Kate rolled her eyes. "What is it with her? We only met her a few days ago and suddenly we can't walk two feet without her getting stuck on the bottom of our shoes."

"Who's Tina Pink?" Alexandra asked.

"One of those planners we mentioned despising," Kate said. "She and Brides by Brianna hold the top spots on our 'most hated' list."

"We thought Brianna was the worst," Mack said. "Until Tina popped onto the scene."

"What did Tina do?" I asked as I heard something slam to the floor in the back.

"Is he cursing?" Kate asked as we heard a series of sounds more roars than words.

Alexandra cocked her head. "I think that's French."

It was only the rarest of occasions when I'd heard Buster or

Mack utter an oath not containing the words "sugar" or "Jiminy Cricket."

Mack flinched. "When he gets really upset, he slips into his high school French." Mack's cheeks reddened. "But he only ever learned the bad words. This was before he joined the Road Riders for Jesus."

Alexandra listened for another second. "His accent's not bad."

Mack rubbed a hand over his bald head. "Tina Pink was hired by one of our longtime clients, but now she's convinced them she can do the flowers for their fiftieth anniversary party."

"Tina does flowers?" Kate made a tsk-ing sound. "I hate when vendors try to annex other people's jobs. I mean, who wants a DJ who also performs your ceremony or a makeup artist who drives your limo?"

I rested a hand on Mack's thick arm. "You know her flowers aren't close to what you and Buster create."

"Of course they aren't," Mack said, nervously tugging on his dark-red goatee. "But by the time the client clues in, we'll have lost the contract. I don't even know if Buster will take them back after they've jumped ship to another florist. You know he can get touchy about those things."

"I'm sure he'll calm down," I said as another crash made us all jump.

"That's it." Buster stomped out from the rear of the shop. "He's fired."

"Who's fired?" Kate whispered.

"Antonio. One of our setup crew." Mack whispered back.

Buster saw us and unclenched his fisted hands. "I'm sorry you had to hear that, ladies. Please excuse my French."

"Literally," Kate mumbled.

Mack rushed up to Buster and rubbed the back of his leather vest. "You need to let it go."

"Don't worry about us," I said to Buster. "We feel the same way about Tina."

He raised his eyebrows and the black motorcycle goggles on his forehead went up with them. "You know her?"

"She tried to steal one of our clients right in front of Annabelle," Kate said, taking Buster by the arm and leading him to a metal barstool.

He put his head in his hands and slumped over the high stainless steel table. "Not only did she steal a client, she also poached one of our best workers. Antonio has been with us for years."

"I think I saw him at The Line yesterday," I said, taking the stool across from Buster. "I thought someone in Tina's crew looked familiar."

"You're right," Kate said. "He's been at all of the weddings we've done together. I can't believe he left you."

"To be clear, he didn't leave." Buster held up a hand. "He was moonlighting with her and thought we wouldn't find out."

"In this tight-knit business?" Alexandra shook her head. "I still hear things, and I live all the way across the pond."

Buster shook a finger in the air. "That delivery to Perry's is the last time he'll ever work for us."

Kate's head snapped in my direction and she mouthed "Perry's?"

"Wait a second," I said. "You two did the flowers for Cher's reception?"

"Someone named Hedda Lettuce ordered them," Mack said. "Were you there? How did they look?"

"Great." I fished around in my purse for my phone. "Remind me again, is Antonio a big guy?"

"Not as big as us, but he's bulky enough to handle our heavy deliveries," Buster said.

"He set up the bar on Saturday, didn't he?" Kate asked.

Buster and Mack both bobbed their heads up and down.

I felt my stomach tighten. "And the uniform the Lush crew wears on-site or to deliver is . . ."

"Black pants and a black long-sleeve Henley with our logo on the front left corner," Mack said. "Why?"

I fished around in my purse for my phone. I needed to call Reese. It looked like we'd found another man in all black who was at the murder scene. Both murder scenes.

CHAPTER 22

"I s it your goal to get everyone else's employees killed or named as a suspect in a murder investigation, or is it a happy accident?" Richard asked, stomping into my apartment with his leather crossbody bag and Hermes in tow. He placed the bag on my couch, and the tiny Yorkie jumped out and began sniffing the upholstery, no doubt smelling crumbs of the cupcakes from earlier in the morning.

I was glad I'd had time, after dropping Alexandra off at her hotel and Kate off at her apartment, to change into yoga pants and a T-shirt and throw my hair into a ponytail. It was better to be comfortable when dealing with one of Richard's meltdowns.

"Why are you complaining?" I shut the door behind him and sat back down on the couch where I'd been going over the paperwork for Debbie and Darla's baby shower. Hermes scampered over to me and put his paws on my leg so he could give my papers a thorough nose inspection. "The guy I told Reese about doesn't even work for you. Antonio works for Buster and Mack. At least he used to."

"I'm being outraged for them." Richard tapped one foot rapidly as he stared me down. "First you get one of my best waiters implicated in the murder. Then he gets killed. Now you've managed to get one of Buster and Mack's employees implicated. Let's hope he doesn't go the same way as Blanche."

I put down the event schedule I was red lining, and Hermes turned around three times before curling up on top of it. "Blanche didn't get killed because I told the cops he might know something."

"Are you so sure? Why else would he have been killed if not to shut him up?"

"I don't know. There's still a chance this is a hate crime and someone is out to get drag queens for no other reason than they're not mainstream."

Richard paused and thought for a moment. "What a sobering thought."

I watched him blink hard a few times, and I wondered if he was thinking he wasn't exactly mainstream. Come to think of it, none of my friends were. I stood up and reached for his hand. "Why don't we have a drink? I think my nerves need a little calming after the past few days."

He sank onto the couch, absently rubbing Hermes's head while I headed for the kitchen. "So why are the cops interested in one of Buster and Mack's guys?"

I looked across the opening between my kitchen and living room. "Wait a second? You read me the riot act before even knowing why Antonio was taken into custody?"

"You know the mantra I live and die by, Annabelle."

"Asking for forgiveness is easier than asking for permission," I said as I pulled my last chilled bottle of sparkling wine out of the fridge.

"You really have been an excellent protégé, you know."

I made a face I knew Richard couldn't see, but it made me feel better. I grabbed a dish towel and two champagne flutes from my cabinets before returning to the living room. "You know how the police were interested in Fern because two witnesses at Perry's claimed to see a man in black messing with the gold velvet before Blanche was strangled behind it?"

Richard took the two glasses from me and inspected them. Hermes did the same. "They didn't really think Fern could have done it, did they?"

I peeled off the gold foil from the top of the bottle and unwound the wire cage sitting over the cork, dropping both on my glass coffee table. "I don't think Reese thought he was a real suspect, but if you'll remember, there weren't many men in black at the reception for Cher Noble."

"Not your typical memorial reception, I suppose."

I draped the yellow dish towel over the cork and twisted the bottle until the cork jumped out with a pop. Hermes yipped in response. "The more I thought about it, though, the more I realized there were other men in black there like the band members in tuxedos. Then Buster and Mack mentioned Antonio's last job for them was delivering the flowers. The Lush uniform is all black."

"You're right," Richard said. "The behind-the-scenes people almost always wear black."

"I know *we* do." Although the black dresses Kate and I wore to work weddings weren't an official uniform, they helped us blend into the crowd and gave us a cohesive look.

I poured sparkling wine into the two glasses Richard held up, waiting for the fizz to settle before filling them up the rest of the way. Hermes sniffed the tops of the glasses and wrinkled his nose. He retreated to the other end of the couch. Richard handed me a glass, and I sat down next to him.

"I don't know if Antonio had anything to do with the murders, but he was at both scenes, so maybe he saw something." I took a small sip, the bubbles effervescing in my mouth.

Richard gave me a pointed look as he held up his glass to mine. "Shouldn't we toast to something?"

"To no more murders?" I suggested.

"How about to not having you implicate any more employees?"

"Ha ha," I said. "How about to Cher Noble and Blanche Davidian?"

Richard pressed his lips together and gave a quick bob of his head. "Gone too soon."

We clinked glasses and drank. I put my glass down on the coffee table and flopped back on the couch cushions as there was a knock on my door.

Richard glanced at his Gucci watch. "Who are you expecting? I'm sure Kate is out on a date by now. She could even be on date number two by this point."

I was going to scold him for making fun of my assistant's active social life, but I knew he wasn't too far off.

He sat up straight, his eyes widening. "Do *you* have a date tonight?"

I shook my head. Reese and I had made no plans to get together, and I thought he was probably busy tracking down the new lead I'd given him. He hadn't been too happy when I'd called him about it, clearly having a hard time believing these clues were falling into my lap.

I cracked the door and felt a little relieved it wasn't him. My relief was short-lived when Leatrice pushed past me, and I heard Richard's groan behind me. I coughed as the unmistakable scent of mothballs followed her inside.

"What are we celebrating?" she asked, spotting the bottle on the table.

I took in her outfit—double-knit plaid bell-bottoms and a rust-colored sweater vest with a brown-patterned scarf tied around her neck—and decided not to ask questions. "Nothing really. We were toasting the two murder victims."

"What in the name of all that's holy are you wearing?" Richard asked, holding a hand over his nose.

I shot him a look, but Leatrice giggled. "Fern went through my closet earlier and said I wasn't taking advantage of all the vintage fashions I have. He said if I was going to have the hair, I might as well complete the look."

Fern had returned Leatrice's hair to the nearly black Mary Tyler Moore flip she'd worn up until last year when she went burgundy and then blond. I understood what he meant. With the hair and the clothes, she really could have stepped right out of the 1970s. I wasn't sure if I thought that was a good thing or not.

Richard reached out and touched the thick fabric of the pants. "These haven't seen the light of day since the Carter administration."

Hermes scurried over, hopping up on the arm of the couch so he could smell Leatrice's clothes. He sneezed twice and ran back to Richard.

Leatrice glanced down at herself. "They might be a bit musty."

Richard gave her an arch look. "You think?"

"Why don't I get you a glass?" I headed for the kitchen, partly to get a glass and partly to escape the mothball cloud.

I opened my fridge, sticking my head inside as I searched for anything decent to serve my guests. I scolded myself for not being better prepared as I scanned the empty shelves. The only time my kitchen was ever stocked was when Richard took pity on me and cooked. I wondered how I could finesse him into invading with bags of groceries again. Finding nothing worth eating, I closed the door, grabbed another champagne flute from the cabinet, and rejoined Richard and Leatrice.

I nearly dropped the glass when I saw Reese standing in the room. "What are you . . .? I didn't know you were coming . . . I mean, I didn't hear you knock."

Reese gave me a half grin. "Leatrice let me in."

He wore jeans and a white T-shirt with a weathered brown leather jacket. A single dark curl fell over one eyebrow. The look was so James Dean I had to remind myself to breathe.

"I heard his footsteps on the stairs." She looked proud of herself as she beamed at the detective.

I continued to be amazed by her hearing. She may have started to forget a few things here and there, but no one walked past her apartment without her knowing. It was the reason I usually took off my shoes when leaving the building.

Leatrice rocked back on her heels. "It looks like this is turning into quite the party."

Richard looked less thrilled as he and Hermes glared at Reese from the couch. I really needed to have a talk with Richard about hiding his feelings better and not turning his dog into such a diva.

I handed Leatrice her glass and jerked a thumb in the direction of my kitchen. "Let me get another champagne flute."

"I'll help you," Reese said, following me as Leatrice and Richard watched, one looking like she'd won the lottery, and the other looking like he'd been forced to wear white after Labor Day.

We stepped into the kitchen, and he spun me around to face him, his hands on my hips. "I wanted to apologize for last night."

I shook my head. "It wasn't your fault. I . . ."

"I shouldn't have talked about work, and I never should have told you about Fern." He lifted one hand to my face and traced his thumb over my bottom lip. "I know how important your friends are to you. I never should have freaked you out."

I would have told him he was forgiven if I'd had the power to speak, but as it was, it took all my energy not to melt to the floor.

Reese leaned over and unfolded one half of the wooden shutters across the divide with the living room so Leatrice and Richard couldn't see us. I heard Richard's sharp intake of breath, and I didn't need to see him to imagine his facial expression. I tried to put Richard out of my mind as Reese bent over and brushed his lips over mine.

"I've been thinking about you all day," he whispered. "I loved hearing your voice when you called me, even if it was about the murder case."

I raised my arms to his neck as he kissed me again, my heart pounding. "I didn't expect to see you tonight," I said, lightheaded when he finally pulled away. "I thought you'd be too busy with the new suspect."

He hoisted me up onto the kitchen counter, and my back bumped against the wooden shutters.

Hermes barked and Richard muttered something I was glad I couldn't decipher.

Reese turned my head and began kissing from my ear down my neck. "I let the guys from District Three take the questioning once we located the suspect doing a setup at The Wharf."

I moaned softly as his words trickled into my brain. I put a hand on his chest. "The Wharf Intercontinental Hotel? What was he doing there?"

Reese kissed down to the hollow of my throat. "Setting up some fancy table to photograph. One of the blondes in charge nearly had a fit when we took him in. Told us we were ruining her shoot and she'd have our badges for it."

"Two blondes?" I asked. "Were their names Brianna and Tina?"

"Sounds right," Reese murmured.

I tried to focus on the hot man kissing my neck, but I couldn't help the irritation I felt about Tina Pink doing another styled shoot at another brand new hotel. And this time with Brianna. I was starting to get the feeling this blonde wasn't as ditzy as she looked.

CHAPTER 23

"I could kill her!" Kate said, shaking one of the bottles of Fiji water with a customized pink-and-white label surrounding us on the floor of my office. "Tina Pink is trying to move in on all the new venues and steal our business."

"Don't forget Brianna was with her last night." I took the bottle from her hand and placed it inside one of the pink boxes I'd already filled with iridescent gold shred.

"I already have plenty of reasons to want to kill Brianna. Now Tina is catching up with her."

Most of the floor around where we both sat Indian style was covered with open boxes for us to fill with baby shower-themed treats. Even though Debbie's shower wasn't a wedding, there were still guests coming from out of town and staying in hotels, so Darla had insisted we do welcome boxes for them.

"Technically we shouldn't be mad at her for hustling." I tried to sound more reasonable than I had felt the night before when Reese had let the information slip. "There's no law against doing lots of styled shoots."

Kate adjusted the spaghetti strap of her black-and-white polka dot shorts romper. "Well there should be. Don't fraud laws cover people pretending they have business when they don't?"

"I'm pretty sure not." I gently laid one of the cellophane-covered pink cake pops with the pink-and-gold-striped stick next to the bottled water.

Kate added a clear plastic box of pink champagne gummy bears to the box. "Too bad. I'd love to see those bottle-blondes get dragged off in handcuffs. Can we get Reese on that?"

I picked a stray piece of gold shred off my jeans. "I think he has his hands full right now."

I thought back to him leaving last night. He'd said he had an early morning today, but I knew Leatrice and Richard making alternating delighted and scandalized noises hadn't made him want to stay.

"So did they arrest Antonio?" Kate asked, reaching for the two mochas she'd brought and handing me one.

"From what little Reese told me, they took him in for questioning." I breathed in the scent of my coffee before I took a sip. I much preferred the aroma of coffee to the actual taste.

Kate raised an eyebrow. "Is he holding out on you?"

I felt my cheeks warm as I flashed back to kissing him in my kitchen. "No comment."

Kate grinned. "You should never play poker, Annabelle."

"Enough about me." I reached up to put my coffee on the glass surface of my white sawhorse desk so it wouldn't tip over on the rug. "How was your date last night?"

She twitched one shoulder up and down. "I'm not so sure about the sous chef. He seems a little young."

"I thought he was around your age." I placed the pink top on our finished box and passed it to Kate so she could tie the white silk ribbon around it. Kate was much better at bows than me.

She stretched the ribbon across the top of the box, ran it underneath, twisted it, and brought it up back around the top.

"Exactly. I'm starting to think guys my age are too young for me. I think I need an older man."

I eyed her. "How much older?"

Kate tied a perfect bow and fluffed up the two loops. "How old is Reese's brother?"

"Daniel? You're still hung up on him after one kiss in Bali?"

Kate winked. "It was a really good kiss. Anyway, he seems more stable than the guys I usually date."

"Since when do you like stable?" I asked. I'd never heard her mention stability as one of the things she looked for in a man. Loaded and built were high up on the list, but stable had never made the top hundred as far as I'd known.

"My tastes are changing." Kate handed the box back to me. "It's not like Daniel doesn't check off a lot of the other boxes. He's definitely hot and has a great body, and I think a few gray hairs at the temples are sexy."

I tied on a calligraphed name tag and set the completed box to the side. "Who are you and what have you done with my assistant?"

"Yoo hoo!" Leatrice's voice drifted down the hall from my front door.

"Doesn't your door lock?" Kate asked.

"It doesn't matter. She made herself a key, remember?"

"Right. The do-it-yourself secret agent kit. She sure got her money's worth."

Leatrice had copied my key, fingerprinted most of the building, and used the rearview spy glasses almost every time she went outside.

Her head poked around the doorframe, her coral-pink lips a stark contrast to her nearly black hair. "That looks like a fun project."

"If you consider filling boxes and tying bows fun, it's a real hoot," Kate said, stretching one of her long bare legs out in front of her.

"Do you have a pink wedding this weekend?" Leatrice asked as she stepped into the room and scanned the pink-and-white objects covering the floor.

Kate looked startled as she took in Leatrice's paisley blouse with high-waisted flare-bottomed pants. She slipped her sunglasses down from the top of her head, no doubt to block some of the glare from the shiny fabric of Leatrice's top.

I shook my head. "A baby shower for a former bride."

Leatrice's eyes opened wide. "Goodness. Baby showers certainly have changed since my day."

Before I could explain this wasn't your typical baby shower or mother-to-be, my cell phone began trilling from where I'd set it on my black office chair. I picked it up and swiped it to answer.

"Hey, babe," Reese said.

"Hey," I said. "I didn't think I'd hear from you this morning. I thought you had a crazy day."

He sighed. "It got a lot crazier when I found out our suspect managed to evade custody last night."

"What? Antonio got away?" I tried to keep my voice calm. "How did that happen?"

Kate and Leatrice both gaped at me, and I motioned for them to keep quiet. If Reese knew they were in the room, he might clam up.

"The car he was being transported in was hit on the way to the station. Right outside the hotel, actually. In all the confusion, it seems he walked off."

"How do you walk off from the back of a detective's car?" I asked.

"Good question. The District Three guys are in pretty deep . . ." His voice dropped. "I need to go. I wanted to tell you so you could keep your eyes open."

"Me? Why?"

"You were the one to finger him as a suspect."

"Does he know that?" Now my voice was less than calm.

"He shouldn't. But after what happened last night, I don't have a lot of faith in the District Three detectives. I want you to be on your guard. I'll call you later."

Before I could ask any more questions, he'd disconnected.

"Did I hear correctly?" Kate asked. "Antonio isn't in police custody?"

"Who's Antonio?" Leatrice asked.

"A suspect in the murder case," I said. "I figured out he was at both crime scenes, and the cops went to pick him up yesterday."

"But he got away?" Leatrice tapped her chin. "That does make him seem more guilty."

"Reese wants me to keep an eye out for him."

"Why? You don't even know him?" Kate asked.

"In case the other detectives let my name slip."

Kate shook her head. "Great. A potential killer might know you gave the police his name?"

"Probably not." I concentrated on my eyelid not twitching. "Reese called me as an extra precaution."

"I don't get it." Kate took a big gulp of coffee. "Why would he run? The police only wanted to talk to him. As far as we know, he didn't even have a motive."

"Maybe he had a motive we don't know about," I said.

"True," Kate said. "We haven't really analyzed the case."

Leatrice clapped her hands together. "Say no more." She turned on her heel, the fabric of her pants flapping around her ankles, and disappeared down the hall, my front door slamming shut behind her.

"What did we say to make her leave so quickly?" Kate asked. "I want to remember so we can say it the next time."

"Who knows? But I don't think she's gone for good." I arranged a water bottle, cake pop, and box of gummy bears in a box and handed it to Kate. "And we still need to finish a dozen of these and get them to The Willard hotel."

I heard my front door open and exchanged a look with Kate.

"She's back," Kate said in a singsong voice.

A large white board with bell-bottom legs appeared in the doorway. "I brought this so we could brainstorm about the case."

Leatrice propped the board against the wall, and I realized it was almost as tall as her. She uncapped a black dry erase marker. "Let's list out the victims first."

"Might as well," I said to Kate as she handed me back a box with a bow. "At least it will kill the time."

"If you say so." Kate slipped her sunglasses back onto the top of her head. "The first victim was Cher Noble."

"Strangled at the wedding," Leatrice added as she wrote Cher's name on one side of the board.

"Blanche Davidian was strangled at the memorial reception for Cher," I said, tying on a name tag and reaching for an empty box.

Leatrice wrote the word 'strangled' under each of their names. "And they knew each other, correct?"

"Yes, they were rivals in the annual Halloween drag races. We thought Blanche might have killed Cher, until she was murdered." I handed Kate a filled box. "Both Blanche and Cher were at our wedding on Saturday, but Blanche claimed to have left early. Other than that, I don't know of any other connections."

Leatrice tapped the end of the marker on her chin, leaving a series of black dots. "So this could be someone out to kill drag queens."

"Cher did think someone was following her the week before the wedding, and she told Fern her car tires had been slashed."

"So Fern had a connection to one of the victims?" Leatrice wrote Fern's name under Cher's.

"But only to Cher," Kate said, inspecting a finished bow before handing the box to me. "And Blanche never said anything about being in danger."

Leatrice gave her head an abrupt shake. "If someone wanted to kill random drag queens, why start with one at your wedding? Wouldn't there be places with more drag queens?"

"Sure," Kate said. "Drag queen brunch at Perry's on Sundays where we found Cher. Also Hotel Rouge once a month on Thursdays, although that's for cross-dressers at all levels."

I stared at her. "How do you know this?"

"I'm plugged in to the social scene in DC," Kate said.

"I had no idea the social scene in DC was so all encompassing," I said.

Kate patted my knee. "You live a sheltered life."

Leatrice bobbed her head, apparently agreeing with Kate.

"So are you saying you don't think the killer was out to get drag queens?" I asked, eager to shift the conversation away from my boring social life and back to the case.

Leatrice tapped her marker on the white board. "Not any drag queen. The killer wanted Cher dead and risked being seen at your wedding to do it. Maybe the second murder was only connected to the first because the killer thought Blanche knew something."

Kate slapped my leg. "Blanche did say she knew something when we talked to her at the reception."

"But she never said what it was, and she was dead a few minutes later," I said, rubbing my jeans where Kate had hit me.

"Interesting." Leatrice underlined Blanche's name. "And the suspect who escaped can be placed at both the reception where Blanche was killed and the wedding?"

"Yes," I leaned back and rested the palms of my hands behind me. "Antonio. He worked for Buster and Mack doing setup and delivery so he was on-site at the wedding and delivered the floral arrangements to Perry's. But aside from opportunity, I can't think of any reason he'd have to kill Cher or Blanche. I can't imagine he knew them."

"What if he didn't have to know them?" Leatrice sucked in air. "What if he was a hit man hired to kill them?"

Kate gasped. "Reese said the murders did look like they were done by someone who knew what they were doing."

I looked from Kate to Leatrice. "Even if I was to somehow believe Buster and Mack inadvertently hired a hit man to work in a flower shop, why would anyone put a hit on two drag queens?"

Leatrice was silent for a minute. "Good question. We need more information about the victims."

"I know exactly where we can get it," Kate said. "Tonight at Hotel Rouge."

I shook my head. "No way. Reese will kill me if he finds out I went to a drag night looking for information about the murder victims. Not to mention Richard. It's the one thing they both have in common."

"Would you rather be killed by Reese or Antonio?" Kate asked, whipping a length of silk ribbon around her neck and making a face like she was being strangled.

"We don't even know if Antonio did it," I said, putting a hand to my throat. "And we certainly don't know if he's a hit man or not."

Kate shrugged. "Have it your way. If it was me who'd fingered a hit man, I'd want to get as much evidence to put him away as possible, but I'm funny that way."

I folded my arms over my chest. "Fine. But I'm only going for half an hour. We are in and we are out."

Leatrice jumped up and down. "This is so exciting. I need to go pick out something fun to wear." She dropped the marker and hurried out of the room.

"Now look at what you've done," I told Kate. "We're stuck taking Leatrice to a drag night."

"Look at the bright side." Kate grinned. "With her clothes and hair, she might be able to pass as a drag queen."

CHAPTER 24

Kate held one side of the glass doors open for me, and we paused inside the Hotel Rouge bar as Leatrice hurried to catch up.

"I'm still not sure this is such a great idea," I said as Leatrice teetered up to us in a rainbow-striped jumpsuit with belled sleeves and flared pants. Since she now came up past my shoulder, I knew she wore some sort of heels under her long billowing pant legs.

Kate took in Leatrice. "It'll be fine. She blends right in."

Kate had a point. Leatrice would fit in with a room filled with drag queens better than I would. I'd worn a pink sequined tank top with my jeans and black cardigan, but Kate had still deemed my outfit too "soccer mom" for a night at a bar. Between her deep V-neck minidress and Leatrice's disco garb, I was feeling a little buttoned-up.

I scanned the narrow space with a white bar across the far end, a red banquette stretching down one wall, and white leather furniture clustered around cocktail tables. The furniture was modern and sleek, the ambient lighting was red, and the music was pulsating. Definitely the hippest hotel bar I'd ever seen. But unlike most bars I'd been in, this one had few men. As far as the eye could see there were short skirts and long legs and big hair. And instead of smelling like beer, this bar held the lingering scent of perfume.

"Should we get a table?" I asked, raising my voice to be heard over the music and motioning to an empty one near the door.

Kate shook her head. "The bar."

We worked our way through the towering women until we reached the curved bar. There was one open barstool, so we hoisted Leatrice up onto it and stood next to her on either side. An attractive bartender in a black T-shirt put a hand to his ear—a signal to yell our drink order to him—which we did.

The blonde next to me with a long neck and pronounced Adam's apple winked and smiled. I pivoted toward Kate. "So who are we looking for exactly?"

Kate swiveled to face the crowd, her dirty martini in one hand. "Do you recognize anyone from Cher's memorial reception?"

"It's hard to say for sure." I ran my eyes over the brightly colored cocktail dresses and plus-size evening suits. "I'd probably recognize dresses before I'd recognize faces."

"That's not good," Kate said. "I don't think anyone would wear the same dress twice in one week."

Leatrice spun around on her barstool, moving the paper umbrella out of her way before taking a sip from her blue frozen drink. "I would love to have some of these dresses."

Leatrice's love of creative clothing went hand in hand with her desire to be a secret agent. I, for one, was grateful she didn't have a closet filled with chiffon and sequins.

"I might recognize hair," I said, switching my wine glass from one hand to the other. "You don't think they would change wigs from a few days ago, do you?"

Kate tapped a finger to her chin. "Fern would be the one to ask."

I shook my head. No way was I dragging Fern any deeper into

things. He'd already been suspected of murder twice this week and considered fleeing the city. I did not want to lose my number one wedding hairstylist to a nervous breakdown.

A brunette in a black satin pantsuit with dramatically smoky eyes and bright-red lips passed us and raised her glass to Leatrice. "Love the jumpsuit, girl."

Leatrice giggled and raised her glass in return. "She certainly has a deep voice doesn't she?"

Kate rolled her eyes to me over Leatrice's head. "Do you remember what Hedda Lettuce looks like?"

"Brown hair, purple eye shadow, Roman nose, slight five o'clock shadow," I said.

"That doesn't narrow it down much," Kate said as a lanky bow-legged blonde with a wispy moustache clomped by us in thigh-high boots.

I turned to the bartender. "Do you happen to know someone by the name Hedda Lettuce?"

He shook his head. "I'm not good with names."

I wanted to ask him how you could forget a name like Hedda Lettuce, but I smiled.

"I know Hedda," Adam's apple next to me said.

I pivoted. "You do? Is she here tonight?"

The blonde didn't answer right away, instead giving me a sultry smile. "Quid pro quo, honey. What's your name?"

"Annabelle," I said.

"I'm Trevor." He extended a hand. "This must be your first time here."

I shook his hand, admiring the pink-polished nails. "Yep. My friends and I are looking for Hedda."

Trevor looked at Kate and Leatrice and fluttered his long lashes at me. "I would have remembered a pretty thing like you."

I wasn't sure what was happening, but I scooted closer to Leatrice. "So Hedda Lettuce?"

"Right." Trevor pointed to a cluster of people a few feet away from us. "In the purple dress and the feathered fascinator."

I leaned over Leatrice and grabbed Kate's arm. "I found Hedda. In the purple dress and feather hair thing."

Kate raised one arm in the air. "Yoo hoo!" she called, her voice rising above the music and the buzz of conversation. "Hedda Lettuce!"

Hedda swung her head toward Kate's voice and beamed when she recognized her. "Look what the cat dragged in."

She ambled over to us, swaying her hips from side to side and gave us each air kisses. Her eyes fell to Leatrice. "What do we have here?"

"This is my neighbor," I explained. "Leatrice."

Hedda handed Leatrice her glossy-purple fingertips. "Hedda Lettuce. Enchanted to meet you. Love the name."

Leatrice giggled again and shook Hedda's fingers. "Nice to meet you, Miss Lettuce."

"We wanted to ask you a few questions about Cher and Blanche," I said, "since you knew them both."

Hedda's face darkened for a moment before she regained her smile. "What do you want to know? I think I told the police everything."

"We think their murders may have been hits," Kate said. "Do you know any reason why someone would hire a hit man to murder them?"

Hedda's purple-lidded eyes widened. "A hit man? Why do you think it was a hit man?"

"The killer left virtually no evidence, which makes us think it was a professional," I said. "Plus, the victims were garroted. That's an old-school mob method."

Leatrice bobbed her head up and down. "Like in *The Godfather*."

"The mob? I can't imagine either Cher or Blanche had

anything to do with the mob." Hedda shivered. "Cher would have told me if she feared for her life because the mob was after her."

I switched gears. "Did you happen to see a man in black at Cher's reception?"

Hedda nodded. "I told the detectives when they interviewed me. I saw someone in all black near the gold velvet. The next time I noticed the fabric, it was down."

So Hedda was one of the two witnesses. "We think we found the man you saw, but he escaped police custody."

"Really?" Hedda pressed a hand to her purple scoop-neck bodice. "And you think that man was a hit man?" She turned around and waved for someone to join us.

A redhead in an emerald-green cocktail dress approached, giving us the once-over and arching a brow. She had an expertly drawn-on beauty mark on her left cheek and wore crimson lipstick.

"This is Rhoda Dendron," Hedda said, waving a hand in front of her. "She was Blanche's roommate, and she also saw the man in all black at Cher's reception."

Rhoda shot Hedda a look but smiled at us. "Who are you?"

"Wedding planners," I said, deciding not to give our names. "Cher was killed at our wedding."

Rhoda's mouth fell open a bit. "I'm sorry. I didn't recognize you at first since you're not wearing your black dresses."

I studied her face. "Do we know you?"

She touched a hand to her bright-red hair. "I'm sure you don't recognize me. I bartend for Richard Gerard Catering."

"You work for Richard?" Kate asked.

"Not for very long," Rhoda shifted from one foot to the other. "David, I mean Blanche, hooked me up and put in a good word for me."

I rubbed one of my temples. "So were you there on Saturday?"

"I was setting up the bar in the tapestry room."

I tried to process the new information. "Did the police question you about knowing both victims?"

Rhoda put a hand on my arm. "Oh, I didn't really know Cher. I mean, I knew Blanche had an issue with her, but that was about it."

"And you and Blanche got along well?" I asked.

Rhoda rolled her eyes. "Blanche was a diva, which was why she and Cher didn't get along. But the two of us got along fine as roommates."

Hedda bobbed her head up and down. "Two divas are too many. Blanche wasn't the only person Cher didn't get along with."

I remembered what we'd heard about Cher and Tina clashing. Tina definitely fell into the diva category, as well.

"Did you see Blanche leave the wedding early?" Kate asked Rhoda.

"I heard about it but didn't see it. I was unloading my liquor behind the bar, and the drama with David and Richard happened downstairs in the prep area."

That meshed with what Richard had told me.

"Do you think you could identify the man in all black you saw at Cher's reception?" I asked.

Rhoda looked at Hedda. "I didn't see a face, did you?"

"No," Hedda said. "Only a back."

"I have a question." Leatrice leaned closer to Rhoda and Hedda. "What kind of mascara do you use to get your lashes so long?"

"These things?" Hedda batted her eyes at Leatrice. "They're as fake as my rack."

Leatrice's eyes darted to Hedda's chest and back to her eyes.

Rhoda reached into her purse. "I always carry a spare pair. Let's go to the bathroom, and I'll get you fixed up."

Leatrice slid off her barstool and disappeared with Rhoda.

Kate hopped up onto the barstool and was instantly taller than me. "I can actually see over a few of the heads." Her face froze. "Uh oh."

I followed her gaze and saw Reese pushing his way through the crowd toward us. He didn't look happy.

"You didn't answer my calls or texts," he said when he reached us.

"Hello, handsome," Hedda said, checking out Reese in his dark jeans and gray T-shirt.

"It's loud in here," I said. "I didn't hear them. Did we have plans?"

He looked around, taking in the number of burly women in cocktail dresses and wigs, and slanting his eyes at me. "I hope you aren't going to try to convince me you happened to pop in here on drag night?" His eyes landed on Hedda. "Weren't you one of my witnesses from Perry's?"

Hedda grinned at him. "I'm flattered you remember me, sweetie."

Reese shook his head at me. "This has reached compulsion level."

"Actually, this was all my idea. I take full responsibility for us being here." Kate held out her wrists. "Take me in and lock me up, Detective."

Hedda held out her own wrists. "Yes, please. You can handcuff me any day."

Reese looked at me, and I could see the side of his mouth twitching. He closed the distance between us and put a hand on my waist. "Do I need to lock you up to keep you out of danger?"

"No." I did my best to sound indignant. "And I'm not in danger." I angled my head at him. "Why aren't you more upset? You normally lose your mind if you think I'm messing around in your investigation."

Reese sighed. "It doesn't seem to have any affect on you, so I've decided not to get mad anymore."

"Really?" I studied him. "What's the catch?"

He leaned in so his lips were brushing my ear. "The catch is

I'm going to be spending a lot more time with you. You can't get into trouble if you're with me."

I felt shivers run through my body, and I leaned back against the bar for support. Now that was a plan I could get behind. "Is your showing up here part of the plan? How did you find me anyway? The only people who knew I was coming here are with me."

"Easy. I tracked your phone."

"Should I be impressed or annoyed you used police resources to keep tabs on me?"

He tilted his head at me. "It's hardly police resources. I added a locator app to your phone."

When my mouth dropped open, he added, "With the amount of trouble you seem to get into, I figured it may save your life one day."

I tried to work up some indignant anger, but I had to admit to myself he was probably right. "So is this part of Operation Annabelle?"

"Is that the code name for our mission tonight?" Leatrice appeared at our shoulders, her face brightening when she saw Reese. "Are you here undercover? Should I pretend I don't know you?"

"If I were you I'd take the offer," I said to him under my breath.

To his credit, Reese didn't appear shocked at Leatrice's appearance even though it looked like a pair of butterflies had died on her eyelids, and her hair was teased so far out from her head no one could stand within two feet of her. Rhoda must have been packing some serious hair product in her bag.

Rhoda held out her fingertips to Reese. "Well, hello handsome."

"This is Rhoda Dendron," I said. "Blanche Davidian's roommate."

Reese shook Rhoda's fingertips. "You're one of the witnesses from Perry's aren't you?"

Rhoda pulled back her hand, her smile flickering.

"I already asked him, but he didn't see a face so he can't tell us if it was Antonio or not," I said.

Kate cleared her throat. "Speaking of Antonio, did you guys locate him yet?"

"We did," Reese said.

"Who's Antonio?" Hedda asked.

"The guy we thought might be the man who was in all black and a hit man who murdered Cher and Blanche," I said.

"We're pretty sure he didn't kill Cher or Blanche," Reese said.

"How can you be so sure?" I asked. "The clues point to him being involved."

"Because we found him floating in the Potomac River," Reese said. "Still wearing the handcuffs he had on when he escaped from the police."

CHAPTER 25

"So let me get this straight," Richard said as he stood in the driveway of Darla's brick McMansion, waving in a delivery truck as it backed up to the garage. "The second person you tipped off the cops to as a suspect was found dead?"

I put my fingers in my ears to block the truck's piercing beeps warning of its reversing. "Why are you making it sound like this is my fault?"

Richard put his hands on his hips and gave me a look telling me I didn't want to know the answer to my question. The sleeves of his lavender button-down were rolled up in crisp folds to his elbows, but he still wore a designer belt with his black pants. I suspected the belt cost more than my entire wardrobe. Since we'd be spending most of the day overseeing the load in and setup for Debbie's baby shower at her mother's home, I'd worn jeans and a white T-shirt with the Wedding Belles logo on the front. Even though Richard rolled his eyes at the branded shirts, I was glad I'd bought them in bulk.

"Antonio's murder proves he had something to do with the first two murders," I said.

"How do you figure?"

"The actual killer clearly wanted to shut him up because Antonio knew something that could implicate them, but how was I supposed to know? He seemed to have a lot of connections to the first two crimes. Which reminds me, why didn't you tell me David's roommate works for you?"

Richard held his palms out, and the truck stopped inches from him. "How is that relevant?"

"Because Rhoda Dendron also was at Cher's memorial reception and happens to be one of two witnesses who saw the person in all black messing with the gold velvet before Blanche was killed." I followed Richard over to a patch of grass where he'd left his clipboard.

"Who's Rhoda Dendron?"

I coughed as I got a whiff of the bug repellant I knew Darla had doused the lawn with so guests wouldn't be bitten by mosquitos. "David's roommate. I met him last night at Hotel Rouge."

"I had no idea my bartender had an alter ego or was at Perry's for Cher's reception." Richard looked up from his clipboard and cocked his head at me. "Wait. You were at Hotel Rouge last night? On purpose?"

"It was Kate's idea to talk to more people who might have known Cher and Blanche. And it worked. We met Rhoda and saw Hedda Lettuce again."

"And are you any closer to finding the killer?" Richard asked as he watched gold ladder-backed reception chairs being carried off the truck.

"No," I admitted. "If Antonio wasn't the man in black untying the fabric, I don't know who it was. The only two people who saw him can't remember seeing his face."

Richard shook his head. "I think your compulsion to solve things is a sickness, Annabelle. Maybe you should quit planning weddings and go work with your boyfriend."

"My skill at solving problems is what makes me such a great

wedding planner," I said. "Do you remember how I stitched a bridesmaid into her dress after the zipper popped or the time I covered the ink stain on a wedding gown with chalk?"

"Fine," Richard sighed. "You're the MacGyver of wedding planners. That doesn't mean you should always go looking for trouble."

"I don't go looking for it," I said. "Trouble finds me."

"Speaking of trouble . . ." Richard motioned to Kate walking across the lawn toward us in a floral print miniskirt and her Wedding Belles shirt knotted at the waist. The heels of her slides sank into the grass with each step, turning her gait into more of a lurch.

Kate handed me a to-go coffee cup when she reached me and leaned on my arm as she pulled her heels out of the ground. "One mocha, as promised." She looked at the pair of box trucks in the driveway. "Are Buster and Mack inside the house?"

I wrapped my hands around the cardboard coffee cuff and let the heat seep into my fingers. "They were the first ones here. Apparently the floral carousel is giving Buster fits."

Kate yawned. "How early did they arrive? I feel like it's the crack of dawn right now."

Richard shook his head. "It's after nine in the morning. Of course, not all of us were out bar hopping last night."

"There was no hopping involved," Kate said. "And you'll be pleased to know I had Annabelle and Leatrice home before midnight."

Richard smirked. "Leatrice went out with you?"

"Don't ask," I said, sipping my mocha and tasting the whipped cream on the top. "We couldn't stop her."

Kate moved her sunglasses from the top of her head to her eyes. "We probably should have stopped Rhoda from giving her that makeover, though."

I cringed. "If she'd stopped with the fake eyelashes, it wouldn't have been so bad."

"What I want to know is how she managed to get Leatrice's hair to stand straight out from her head."

"I think Rhoda was packing hair product in her purse," I said. "And it must have been some sort of cement because Leatrice's hair hadn't gone down any when Reese and I saw her this morning."

Richard turned slowly toward me. "Reese? Why was Reese with you this morning?"

"He found me at the bar last night to tell me about Antonio and was nice enough to give Leatrice and me a ride home." I met Richard's eyes even though I felt my face flush.

"I see how it is." Richard sniffed. "You've moved on. You don't need Richard anymore since you have tall, dark, and testosterone."

"Don't be ridiculous . . ." I began, but he held up a hand.

"I get it. I'm out and he's in." Richard's voice broke. "I remember when you would have invited me to go hunting for suspects with you. I guess now you have *him*."

"But you complained the entire time," I said. "You hate being dragged into investigations."

"Complaining is part of my charm, Annabelle," Richard said. "You know that. Anyway, even if I didn't want to do it, I did it for you."

I reached for his arm. "I'm sorry. I didn't know you felt left out."

"It's always nice to be asked." He flicked my hand off his arm and flounced off into the open garage.

Kate gave a low whistle. "Your work husband is not happy about your new boyfriend."

"Tell me about it. And my new boyfriend is not happy we keep giving him suspects who wind up murdered."

Kate nudged me. "So did I hear correctly? He left your apartment this morning?"

I ignored her leer. "It's his new strategy to keep me out of trouble. If he's with me he figures I can't be running around getting in trouble."

"You know Richard's right, though. He used to consider it his job to keep you out of trouble the same way." She raised an eyebrow. "Not exactly the same way, but you know what I mean. I'm guessing Richard's babysitting involved a lot more snark and a bit more cooking."

I thought back to Richard sleeping over at my place after someone had broken in and ransacked it, even though my back door lock was broken. He'd constructed a wall of bells—favors for a wedding—to alert us in case the burglars returned and had made me breakfast the next morning.

"I'll fix it," I said. Even though I was pretty into Reese, I did not want to lose my best friend over him. "There has to be a way to make Richard happy without dumping Reese."

Kate patted me on the back. "Tell me if you figure it out."

I pulled my phone out of my jeans pocket and inspected the weather app, feeling relieved when I saw the forecast for sunny skies on Saturday. A lot of our design for the baby shower relied on us using the backyard pool deck. As good as a rain plan was, it was always a last resort.

"And here I thought this was a good neighborhood." The voice made me snap my eyes up from my phone.

"What is she doing here?" Kate said, not bothering to lower her voice even though the spot where Tina Pink stood on the sidewalk in front of Darla's house was well within earshot.

Tina put a hand on the waist of her spandex running tights. "I live here. I thought you two lived in the district."

I noticed Tina's thighs didn't touch and the part of her stomach exposed by her black sports bra was completely flat. More reasons not to like her.

"You live in this neighborhood?" I asked, purposefully not answering her question. The sprawling mansions with wide yards and the occasional gated entrance were not typically where twenty-somethings in the DC area lived. Especially not newbie wedding planners.

Tina flipped her blond ponytail and pointed to the cream-colored house across the street with a pair of curved staircases leading up to the front door and an actual turret on one side. I remembered her mentioning moving into a big new house, but I hadn't imagined she'd meant *this* big.

"What does her husband do again?" Kate asked, this time so only I could hear. "I know she doesn't make enough money planning weddings to afford a chateau."

I searched my memory. "Nightclubs, I think. Tina mentioned it when we saw her doing that styled shoot. She said he was a bigwig."

"I don't think she was exaggerating."

I watched as a black Mercedes sedan glided past us and turned into Tina's driveway. She turned without a backward glance at us and bounced up to the car, throwing her arms around the stocky, dark-haired man who emerged. He wound an arm around her waist, and I saw the glint of a gold watch on his wrist and more than one ring on his hand.

"She's taller than him," Kate whispered. "And younger."

"Does it surprise you at all Tina is a gold digger?" I asked, watching as her thick-necked husband glanced over at us as Tina said something in his ear and looked away again.

"Nope." Kate said. "I'm pretty sure if you look up 'trophy wife,' you'll see Tina's picture."

"Jealous?" I asked.

"Not at all. He's way too *Jersey Shore* for me." Kate winked at me. "I'm not worried. I know one day my sugar daddy will come."

"I think the expression is 'one day my prince will come.'"

Kate seemed to consider this for a moment. "You say it your way, I'll say it mine."

My phone buzzed in my hand, and Reese's name popped up on the screen.

"Did you leave something at my place?" I asked when I answered, angling my body away from Kate and lowering my voice.

"No," he said, his voice also quiet. "But thanks for letting me stay over."

My cheeks warmed. "Of course. It was my . . . I mean, anytime." I was glad he couldn't see my face go from faint flush to burning embarrassment.

"Do you happen to know where Richard is this morning?" His voice shifted from flirty to all business.

"Richard? He's here with me, setting up for the baby shower tomorrow. Why?"

"I need to talk to him about David's roommate, the one I met last night."

"Rhoda Dendron? What about him?" I turned back to face Kate and saw her brows raised in surprise.

"Rhoda's legal name is Matt McKee."

"Okay, why do you need to talk to Richard about Matt?"

"I thought he looked familiar last night. Even though he'd made it into a beauty mark, the mole on his cheek reminded me of a photo I'd seen."

My stomach tightened. "What kind of photo?"

"Matt McKee is wanted in Florida for fraud. Mostly stealing credit cards, but he has a rap sheet longer than my arm."

I tried to swallow but my mouth was dry. Was he telling me Richard's bartender and Blanche's roommate was a convicted criminal? I walked to the edge of the lawn so the guys unloading the trucks wouldn't overhear me. "Are you telling me you think he's the killer?"

CHAPTER 26

"So is the detective on his way?" Kate asked, joining me at the end of the driveway after I'd slipped my phone into my jeans pocket.

"How much did you hear?"

"Well, you kind of yelled some of your end of the conversation."

"Sorry. I was startled." I rubbed my bare arms as the sun slipped behind a cloud. "But, yeah, he's on his way here now. He sounded pretty sure about this guy, who apparently has a record."

Kate hooked her arm through mine. "Why don't we go inside until the police arrive? You look like you could use a drink."

"It isn't even ten a.m.," I said as we walked toward the front door of the house. "I mean, I know we're at Darla's house and she's probably drunk, but I don't think booze is the answer."

"Suit yourself." Kate pointed to my paper cup. "We could make your coffee Irish and no one would ever know."

I took a sip of the now lukewarm mocha and opened one side of the wood double doors, stepping into the massive foyer with a sweeping ceiling and a crystal chandelier that would look at home in Versailles. A drop cloth covered the marble floor, and orange

buckets filled with fresh flowers sat around a wire and oasis struc-
ture resembling a carousel complete with four horses.

Mack straightened up from where he bent over the leg of one
of the horses, inserting white roses. "I don't know how they do it
for the Rose Parade. We only have a six-by-eight carousel and
we're using over a thousand roses."

Even though only the bottom third of the wire form was filled
with flowers, I could tell it was going to be stunning. "I can't
believe you guys are actually building a floral carousel."

"Can I ride one of the horses?" Kate asked.

Buster looked up from his crouching position where he was
cutting flower stems. "Don't even think about it."

I inhaled deeply. One benefit of using a thousand roses—the
amazing scent. "The flowers will stay fresh until tomorrow?"

Mack pointed to the spongy green oasis. "The stems are all
going into the oasis, which is soaked with water and our floral
solution. And we'll spray the entire thing once we've finished."

I took a few steps and put a hand on Mack's leather-clad
shoulder. "I'm really sorry about Antonio." Reese had let me call
them the night before and give them the news.

Mack patted my hand. "It's not your fault, honey. He was
clearly mixed up in some unpleasant things."

"I'm sorry we didn't see through him sooner," Buster said,
standing up to his full six and a half feet. "He worked for us for a
long time."

"You always see the good in everybody. That's not a bad thing."
I didn't tell them I wasn't so sure he'd been mixed up in anything
nefarious. I didn't want to admit my suspicions had been so
off base.

"Is that you, Annabelle? Kate?" Darla's voice warbled in from
somewhere in the back of the house.

"Duty calls," Kate said, waving at Buster and Mack as we left
them in the foyer.

We followed the sound of clinking ice cubes down a hall and

into the kitchen where Darla sat at her black granite counter munching on a stalk of celery. I felt confused by the vegetable until I noticed the Bloody Mary in her other hand. She wore a leopard print robe and swung her legs from a white bar stool as she peered out the glass walls overlooking her pool deck.

"We didn't expect you to be up," I said, knowing Darla loved to sleep in. Some might call it sleeping it off.

Darla waved her celery. "I love to watch a party come together. Do you see what they're doing to the pool?"

I looked outside where our lighting company had erected a pink-and-white striped pole extending high out of the center of the pool. Pink swaths of fabric draped from the center pole to shorter poles along the sides of the pool. Even though only half the pool was completed, I knew it would soon look like the top of a carousel.

"It's going to be beautiful," I said. "Are you sure you don't want to wait until it's done so you'll get the full 'wow' factor?" I'd always felt watching party setup was like watching someone get dressed. It took away a little of the magic.

She shook her head as she slid off the barstool. "What else do I have to do?" She picked up a highball glass and headed for a pitcher filled with tomato-red liquid. "Can I get you a Bloody Mary?"

"Thank you, but no," I answered for Kate and myself before Kate could speak. "We have a lot of work to do."

I spotted Richard walking across the pool deck and started for the kitchen door leading outside. I still needed to warn him before Reese showed up. Richard did not react well when he felt he was being ambushed.

"I didn't know you knew my neighbors," Darla said as she poured herself a Bloody Mary and stuck her half-chewed celery on the top.

It took me a moment to realize she meant Tina Pink. "We don't really. I mean, she's a colleague."

"At best," Kate added. "We only met her a week ago."

"She called here a few minutes ago to ask if we were having a party and mentioned she knew you," Darla said, swirling her celery around in her drink. "I forget her name."

"Tina," Kate said with obvious disdain.

"That's right. I knew it was something like that." Darla took a long swig of her drink. "We don't usually get their type around here."

Tina was about thirty years younger than most of the Potomac wives I'd met and significantly less polished. Where Darla was St. John suits and designer highlights, Tina was Fredericks of Hollywood and bleached extensions. It was no wonder Darla didn't like her. I couldn't help smiling a little at my client's reaction. If I'd ever worried about my wealthy clients jumping ship for T Pink, I knew now my fears had been unfounded.

"I get the feeling there's no love lost between you, am I right?" Darla asked.

For someone who was perpetually soused, she had decent radar. "Why do you say that?"

"She wasn't flattering about you on the phone." Darla gave a small shake of her head. "She told me I should give her all my future business."

Kate muttered a few curses under her breath.

Darla drained her glass. "Don't worry, girls. You know I've been thrilled with everything you've done for my Debbie. And I promise you I would never hire someone like her. And I'll make sure my friends don't, either."

I felt a rush of affection for the boozy mom and a little silly for ever feeling threatened by Tina. I'd always believed working hard and focusing on your own business instead of worrying about what everyone else was doing was the key to success. I was grateful Darla had reminded me I was right.

Richard stuck his head into the kitchen from the glass door. "A quick question when you have a moment, Annabelle." He turned his gaze to Darla. "Can I fix you another pitcher of Bloody Marys?"

Darla giggled. "Aren't you a doll? I'm fine for now. You three run along and take care of things."

Kate and I followed Richard out to the pool deck, skirting a ladder and a stack of plastic glass racks. When he turned I could see he had his Yorkie, Hermes, tucked under his arm.

"Darla said it was fine to bring him, and he could do with a pool day," Richard said when I reached out and patted the dog on the head. I saw the dog's setup—a collection of designer squeaky toys and a cashmere blanket draped over his Burberry dog bed—on a nearby lounger chair.

"Does he like to swim?" Kate asked.

Richard arched one brow. "Not without his suit and his floaties."

I could only imagine the designer bathing suit Richard had for his dog. I tried to bring my focus back to the matter at hand and not on the distinct possibility Richard and his dog had matching swimsuits.

"Doesn't Darla have a dog?" Kate asked, twisting to peer around the pool deck.

"He's out being groomed," Richard said. "She wants him looking his best for tomorrow."

"Too bad." Kate rubbed Hermes under the chin. "You'd like a friend to play with, wouldn't you? Someone more fun than Mr. Fussy Pants."

Richard made a face at Kate and put Hermes down in his dog bed.

"I need to tell you something," I said before Richard could zing one back at Kate.

"Well, it's going to have to wait." Richard tapped his foot on the concrete. "We have a major issue."

I glanced around to see if Reese had arrived without me knowing. "Which is?"

"The pink-and-white striped ties I ordered for the waiters to wear were accidentally shipped to Washington state instead of Washington DC," Richard said in one long breath before gasping for air. "They won't be here on time."

I exchanged a relieved look with Kate. "That's not a big deal."

"Not a big deal?" Richard staggered back a few steps. "We've been coordinating this party for months. I can't have my waiters be the only non-custom element. I hope you aren't suggesting they wear tuxedos for an afternoon garden party."

"Would that be the end of the world?" Kate asked. "They could wear the black vests and not the jackets."

"Just the vests?" Richard said, inhaling sharply as Hermes yipped. "Richard Gerard Catering is known for exquisite detailing. I will not have my waiters dressed like they work at an airport hotel."

"I promise you this is not a big deal," I said. I knew this would be nothing compared to learning his bartender was wanted for fraud. "By the way, you have backup bartenders, right?"

Richard slanted his eyes at me. "Matt is my best and works all my top parties including this one. Why do you ask?"

"No reason," Kate said, shooting me a warning look. "Why don't I go online and see if I can find some ties that can be overnighted to us?"

"Good luck finding ones not rayon or polyester," Richard muttered as Kate took out her phone. "It took me weeks to track down the perfect fabric."

I walked Richard a few feet away from Kate, ignoring her looks. I had to tell him about Matt before Reese showed up. "Listen. I need to tell you something you're not going to like."

Richard's expression became solemn, and he set Hermes on a nearby chaise lounge chair. "Does this have to do with that detective?"

I paused before thinking how to respond to him so he wouldn't stomp off in a huff. I looked past his shoulder to where a long white bar was set up on the other side of the pool. I blinked a few times as I saw a tall man turn around from where he was arranging bottles on a back shelving unit. The beauty mark was gone, but I was pretty sure I could make out the mole on his left cheek.

"Is Matt here today?" I asked, hearing my voice crack.

Richard twisted around to follow my gaze. "I had him come so he could inventory the bottles and have the bar set up so we only have to set out glasses in the morning."

My eyes went from Matt, to the glass wall where Darla sat watching us, to Richard. Pink-and-white-striped ties were about to be the least of our problems.

CHAPTER 27

"Bad news," Kate said, walking up to where Richard and I stood on the pool deck.

I had yet to tell Richard my boyfriend was on his way to question his best bartender, and I wondered if I should not tell him at all. Maybe I could finesse it so he didn't see Reese or know Matt was a possible suspect. I knew this probably wasn't my best idea, but neither was letting Richard have a complete meltdown in front of the client.

"No ties?" Richard asked, but didn't look surprised. He stepped back as one of the lighting crew passed us carrying a ladder, and a waiter rolled a stack of plastic glass racks behind him on a dolly, the wine glasses rattling from the bumps in the paving stones. Between the linens being draped onto tables and the lounge furniture being moved into place, the area was slowly starting to come together.

"No," Kate said. "But I did find some pink-and-white-striped fabric."

"And that will help us how?" Richard looked from Kate to me. "I don't suppose you two have sewing skills you've been hiding?"

I shook my head. My sewing knowledge extended to stitching

a hem or replacing a button, two things I'd had to do many times on the job. I knew Kate's skills were right there with mine, so I had no idea where this was going.

"DC Rental has a sewing department, right?" Kate asked. "They've done custom napkins for us at the last minute and even whipped up an extra tablecloth the day before an event."

"You think they'll cut and sew ties for us?" I asked.

Richard nodded slowly as he seemed to warm to the idea. "I don't see why not. I send them tons of business." He pulled out his phone. "Let me call Liz and see if I can sweet-talk her into helping us out."

While Richard stepped aside to call his account rep at the rental company, I looked over at the bar. No Matt. I scanned the pool deck and cursed. "Reese is going to kill me."

"Because you didn't warn Richard?" Kate walked over to a high-top table and straightened the bubble-gum-pink cloth draped over it. "I don't think it matters much. Richard's going to have a hissy fit either way."

"Not that," I said, although I did think Richard would react worse to Reese appearing at his setup than he would to my explaining everything first. "I lost track of his suspect."

Kate looked around. "Who?"

I pointed to the bar on the other side of the pool. "Matt, aka Rhoda Dendron, was here setting up the bar and now he's gone."

"Unless he has supersonic hearing and managed to overhear us talking about him from the front lawn, I doubt he's made a run for it," Kate said. "Maybe he took a break."

I tucked a loose strand of hair back into my ponytail. "You're right. I'm overreacting. He's probably inside."

Kate patted my arm. "Don't worry. You spend a lot of time with Richard. His overreacting was bound to wear off onto you."

"Hallelujah," Richard said, joining us with a smile on his face. "Life as I know it is not over."

Kate gave me a "what did I tell you?" look.

Luckily, Richard didn't catch the look and continued to talk. "Not only is Liz going to make the ties for me, she's going to go buy the fabric. I feel like I got a last-minute stay from the executioner."

Leave it to Richard to equate not having custom ties for a party to death.

"Glad I could help," Kate said.

"Yes, well," Richard stammered. "I don't know how you thought of it, but it was an excellent idea. I apologize for the many times I've implied all your brainpower goes toward picking up men."

"Was that a thank you?" Kate asked me.

"It was Richard-style," I said. "A little sweet and a little more snark."

"I beg your pardon," Richard said with a sniff. "When am I ever snarky?"

Kate and I did not get the chance to answer him. A series of loud car horns made us all jump.

"I hope the delivery trucks aren't getting jammed up." Richard wrung his hands. "I probably shouldn't have tried to have so many come within the same window of time."

We all ran around the side of the house with the garage. The two white box trucks were still backed up and unloading in the driveway, so I knew they weren't the ones making the noise. I spotted a new truck which had pulled up in front of the house—the liquor truck from the look of the boxes coming off it—and two cars in a face-off trying to get around it.

"Did you know Fern was coming?" Kate asked me.

"That can't be him," I said, taking a few steps closer before I recognized his dark hair pulled back in a low ponytail. He was sitting half out of his white convertible, with his head poking above the windshield, as he waved for the other car to move out of the way. "Nope. You're right. Definitely Fern."

Who else would wear a white button-down shirt topped with

a pink-and-white-striped vest, a pink bow tie, and a straw hat wrapped with a pink ribbon?

Richard threw his arms up. "I can't find pink-and-white ties but he finds a vest?"

I glanced at the other car and my stomach fell. Tina Pink glared through the window of the black Mercedes as she blared her horn.

"Well, this isn't good." Kate looked over her shoulder toward the house. "How do we explain this if Darla comes out here?"

I noticed the guys unloading the trucks had all stopped to gawk at the traffic jam spectacle, and a few waiters wandered around from the back of the house. Pretty soon we'd have the entire neighborhood watching.

"Come on." I waved for Kate to follow me. "We need to put on our negotiator hats."

When I reached Fern's car, I leaned my arms on the side. "Nice outfit."

For Fern, coordinating his outfit with the event—even if he wasn't a guest—was an art form.

He glanced over at Kate and me, and his expression changed from determined to delighted. "Hey, girls! Do you like it? I wore it to see if it worked with the decor before I officially debuted it tomorrow. How's setup going?"

"Good," I said. "What are you doing here?"

Fern gave a quick beep of his horn. "Darla has a new idea for her hair and wants me to do a trial run. I was about to pull in front of the truck, when this two-bit hussy flew up and blocked me."

I caught a glimpse of Tina hunched over her steering wheel, her knuckles white and her face red. "Why does she seem to hate you so much?"

"Is it because of us?" Kate asked, giving Tina a finger wave.

"Not unless you also refused to do her hair when she called you for an appointment," Fern said.

My mouth dropped open. "You did what?"

"She called the other day begging for an appointment." Fern waved a hand in the air. "I suppose she heard I do all the Potomac wives, so she figured if she'd bought into the neighborhood she should be able to use the same hairdresser."

"And you said no?" I asked.

"I didn't like her attitude." He blew her a kiss. "Or her telling me I should stop working with you and start doing weddings for her. I told her I'd never work for her and neither would any other decent stylist. I told her she should stay with SuperCuts."

"Ouch," Kate said.

I would have felt bad for Tina if she hadn't been trashing me to Fern and trying to steal him away. As it was, I had no sympathy for her.

"You know I'm completely on your side," I said. "But don't you need to do Darla's trial?"

Fern motioned to his backseat and the black bag jammed with hair product and brushes. "Send her out here. I'll do her trial in the car."

I looked to Kate for assistance, but her face was blank.

"Back to work, people," Richard yelled, clapping his hands. "This party isn't going to set up itself."

None of the delivery guys moved, so Richard started wrestling with one of the dollies filled with plastic crates himself. I noticed Tina's husband step out of their front door and walk across the lawn as he took in the situation. Even from a distance I could tell he was a good twenty years older than his wife and had at least a hundred pounds on her. A thick gold chain around his neck glinted in the sunlight as he shoved his hands deep into his pants pockets.

Fern looked over at him and back at Tina.

"Is there anything I can say to convince you . . ." I began, but had to step back as Fern threw his car in reverse and flew back, reversing into a spot on the other side of the mailbox.

Tina gunned her car, her tires squealing as she accelerated by us without a second glance. The delivery guys resumed hauling boxes out of the trucks, and Richard let go of the dolly and hurried back around the side of the house.

"Chop, chop, people," he called out behind him. "I'm not paying overtime."

Fern parked his car and got out, hoisting his bag of equipment onto his shoulder. His face was grim as he walked toward us, casting a glance at Tina's husband still standing on the front lawn. "I don't like the look of that guy."

"I mean, any guy who would marry Tina can't be great," Kate said as the three of us headed for the house.

"I would have been happy for you to stay out there all day," I lied. "But I didn't want Reese to see that."

Fern's face brightened a bit. "Is the hot detective here?"

"Not yet. He's on his way." I walked around a stack of liquor boxes by the front door. My phone buzzed, and I pulled it out of my pocket.

"Who is it?" Kate asked.

"Stefan is texting me."

"Doesn't he know the wedding is over? We've broken up. Move on."

I laughed. "Apparently not. He wants to do an 'event autopsy.' His words."

Kate made a face. "That sounds horrifying in so many ways."

I typed quickly on my screen. "I'm telling him I'm at an event setup in Potomac and can't meet with him until next week."

"When he's on his honeymoon? Good thinking."

"Don't he and Jesse live somewhere near here?" Fern asked.

I pressed send. "I think you're right. We always met them downtown, but they moved to Potomac at some point during the planning." I felt relieved our grooms hadn't witnessed the scene with Tina. If I knew Stefan, he wouldn't have thought twice about stopping to rehash the wedding in the middle of the street.

Kate took Fern's bag from him and gasped. "What do you have in here?"

Fern tugged the front of his striped vest. "Hairdryers, curling irons, spray, serum, cement. Everything I might need."

"Hair cement or literal cement?" Kate shifted the bag from one shoulder to the other as she staggered up the brick stairs.

He giggled and gave her a playful shove, almost sending her sprawling back down the stairs. "Aren't you a hoot?"

I caught Kate's arm and steadied her, taking one handle of the heavy bag so the weight was distributed evenly between us.

"So is hot cop coming here on a social call, or is it official police business?" Fern asked.

I ignored his knowing look as the front door opened. "He's coming to interview a new suspect. Richard's bartender, Matt—also known as Rhoda Dendron—was Blanche's roommate and has a record." I looked up and saw the very person I was talking about standing in the doorway.

The bartender's mouth dropped, and he slammed the door closed on us.

"How rude," Fern said, adjusting the tilt of his straw hat.

I grabbed for the door handle and tugged hard, but it was locked. "That was the suspect."

CHAPTER 28

"So much for the element of surprise," I said as I jiggled the knob again.

"That was Rhoda Dendron?" Fern asked. "I feel like I've seen him somewhere before."

"I'm sure you have." I pounded on the wooden door, my hand smarting but not making much of an impact. "He was tending bar at the wedding on Saturday and was at Cher's memorial reception."

The wooden door opened and Mack stood inside holding a pair of floral clippers in one hand. "I thought you were out back."

I stepped inside the foyer and dropped my side of the bag filled with hair products. Kate did the same and the bag thudded onto the marble floor.

Since we'd last seen it, the floral carousel had become significantly more floral. Three of the four horses were completely covered with tightly packed blooms and fewer buckets filled with flowers covered the drop cloth. The bodies of the horses were white and each wore an intricately patterned floral saddle in pastel shades with gold rope reins running from the mouths.

Fern gave a low whistle as he reached a hand out to touch one of the horses.

"Hands off," Buster said, spraying Fern with a water bottle from where he balanced on top of a stepladder. "These need to stay fresh until tomorrow and the oils on your hands do not help."

"Touchy." Fern flicked the water off his hand and a few cold drops hit my arm.

"Did you two see where the guy who opened the door a few seconds ago went?" I asked.

"The one who was carrying in the bottles of liquor?" Mack asked. "He went back out toward the kitchen."

As I'd suspected. I was glad he hadn't made a run for it up the stairs. I did not feel comfortable searching the client's bedrooms.

"If you see him come back through here, don't let him leave," I said.

Mack's face lit up. "Should we tackle him?"

My mind went back to the last time Buster and Mack had helped us by tackling someone. The person had nearly ended up in the hospital. "Try to avoid tackling."

Mack's smile vanished.

"Does this have anything to do with the commotion out front?" Buster asked.

"I was coming to ask the same question," Darla said from the top of the sweeping staircase, a Bloody Mary in each hand.

"Nothing to worry about," Fern said. "I had a little disagreement with your neighbor." He eyed her drinks. "I hope one of those is for me, honey."

Darla looked at both drinks as if deciding which one to give up. "If you mean the horrible people across the street, be careful. The husband runs around threatening anyone his wife gets angry at. Our poor gardener was thrown against his truck for waking her with his weed whacker."

Kate's eyes rested on Fern, darting away before she exchanged a look with me. I knew she was thinking the same thing I was—Fern was no match for Mr. Thick Neck.

Mack followed Kate's eyes and leaned over to us. "Don't worry. We'll watch out for him."

"Thanks." I squeezed Mack's arm.

One nice thing about having friends who looked intimidating enough to belong to a motorcycle gang—no one needed to know the toughest thing their Christian biker gang did was activate their prayer chain.

"If you're okay, we need to run and take care of a few things," I said to Darla.

She waved a hand and sloshed some Bloody Mary onto her wrist. "Of course. Go." She began teetering down the stairs. "I thought I'd get my hair done in the kitchen so Fern and I could watch the rest of the setup."

I motioned for Fern to follow me as I led the way to the back of the house. "You have good light by the bay window."

When we reached the kitchen, I looked out the glass, scanning the pool area for Matt. I didn't see him, but I saw the door to the pool house standing open. It hadn't been open when I'd been outside earlier.

"Come on," I said to Kate. "Let's go find the suspect before Reese gets here and finds out we had him and lost him."

Fern heaved his bag onto a barstool. "I'll watch all the fun from here."

"What's all this 'we?'" Kate said, stepping to the outside through the door I held open. "You aren't throwing me under the bust, are you?"

"No." I tried not to draw a mental picture. "I'm definitely not throwing you under the *bus*."

Hermes ran up to us as we walked onto the pool deck, sniffing around our feet before disappearing again. This meant Richard was near, although I couldn't hear his shrieks—a sign things were going well.

The pool décor had been finished, and the pink fabric now created a high canopy resembling the top of a carousel. It was high enough so light came through and hit the blue water in slats, and we could easily see under it to the other side of the pool and the long white bar where stacks of cardboard liquor boxes remained. It seemed clear Matt had abandoned his bar setup.

We were close enough to the pool to smell the chlorine and see a few leaves floating on the surface. I made a mental note to fish out all the leaves before the party started the next day.

"So where did he go if he came out this way?" Kate asked, watching the staff unfurl pink linens over the cocktail tables.

I pointed to the open glass door. "Maybe he's hiding in there."

Kate ran a hand through her bob. "Unless there's a back door, that doesn't seem like a great escape plan."

She had a point. "Okay," I said. "Why don't you run around the front of the house and make sure he isn't there, and I'll pop my head in the pool house?"

Kate and I split up, and I headed for the brick building—a scaled-down version of the big house. I knew it wasn't too scaled back, especially for a pool house, because it had a living room, kitchenette, bedroom, and full bathroom. All decorated as lavishly as the main house.

I pushed open the glass-paned French doors and stepped inside. The lights weren't on, but since the walls of the living room were glass, it was still bright inside. "Hello?" I called out. "Matt?" I paused and was met with silence. "Rhoda?"

The living room had a pair of white sofas covered in a heavy twill fabric and a coffee table of silvered distressed wood topped with a glass bowl of sand dollars I knew had been purchased, not collected. A unit of built-in cubbies by the door held turquoise beach towels and baskets filled with flip-flops and pool toys.

Hermes appeared in the doorway and scampered past me, sniffing the space until he reached the bathroom door. Then he began yipping. The door opened and Matt emerged, edging himself along the wall.

"Call off your dog," he cried.

I glanced down at the tiny black-and-brown dog inspecting Matt's pant leg. "You're afraid of that?"

"I'm not a dog person," he said, cringing as Hermes sat back on his haunches and looked up at him, his little pink tongue hanging out of his mouth.

I made kissing noises and scooped up Hermes when he ran to me but kept myself positioned in front of the door. "Do you want to tell me why you ran when you opened the door?"

"You said the cops were coming for me, and I was a suspect." He touched a hand to his receding hairline, and I saw a glimpse of Rhoda in the movement. "I freaked."

"Why didn't you mention your record?" I patted Hermes on the head as he wiggled in my arms.

He put one hand on his hip. "Would you bring that up if you were me?" He swirled his hand in the air. "It was a long time ago, and I was a foolish kid. I've tried to put it behind me."

"So you're telling me you had nothing to do with either murder?" I asked.

"Of course not. Why would I?" He took a step closer to the door, keeping his eyes on Hermes. "I'm happy to talk to the police when they arrive."

Kate ran into the room and stopped as quickly as she'd entered. "No sign of . . .Oh, you found him."

"Her attack dog found me," Matt said.

"Attack dog?" Kate's eyes surveyed the room, finally landing on Hermes. "Do you mean him?"

"He's not a dog person," I explained.

Fern rushed into the room and smacked into Kate, sending her stumbling into me. Hermes yipped as I caught myself on the arms of one of the couches, and Matt backed away with his arms in the air.

"Thank heavens I found you," Fern said, trying to catch his breath.

"It's okay," Kate said, straightening up. "We found the suspect."

"And aren't you supposed to be with Darla watching the setup from the kitchen window while you do her hair?" I asked.

"That's why I'm here." Fern put a hand on Kate's arm and leaned into her. "I saw him."

"It's okay." I motioned to Matt. "We found him."

Fern waved both hands in front of himself. "Not him. I realized who I recognized."

"What are you talking about?" Kate said. "Are you sure you didn't inhale too much hairspray?"

"No." Fern leaned against Kate. "I'm certain of it. I saw him at Perry's. It didn't click until today when I saw him."

"Who?" I asked, starting to think maybe Kate had been right about the hairspray.

"I think he means me." A low voice made us all turn toward the back of the pool house.

CHAPTER 29

Tina's husband walked out from the short hallway leading to the bedroom, and Hermes began growling.

"I guess there is a back door to this place," Kate said, taking a step back and bumping into Fern.

"I don't understand." I looked from the dark-haired man to Fern.

"I'm Sal." He bared his teeth in a forced smile. "I wanted to have a little chat with your friend about what happened earlier."

"You mean with the cars?" I glanced at Fern, and he jerked his head to one side while winking. Either he was having a stroke or he was trying to tell me something.

"Yeah." Sal took another step forward and pointed a beefy finger at Fern. "Your buddy with the ponytail there made my wife upset. I don't like it when people make my wife upset."

Matt scooted around so he was standing closer to me, obviously deciding his chances were better with Hermes than with Sal.

"Why don't we do this?" Fern said. "You send your wife in to see me, and I'll give her some highlights that won't look so brassy. While I'm at it, I can do something with your pompadour. On the house."

Sal blinked a few times, and I knew he was trying to figure out if Fern had insulted him. He scratched his head, and I noticed the flash of his pinky ring. Where had I seen a pinky ring lately?

I gasped out loud as things shifted into place for me.

"That's what I was trying to tell you," Fern whispered to me. "He's the man in black."

"Wait, what?" Kate's head snapped in Fern's direction.

I motioned to Sal and nudged Matt. "Could this have been the guy you saw near the gold velvet at Perry's?"

He looked startled but turned to Sal and narrowed his eyes while he studied him. "Definitely. He's the right size, and I remember the guy had dark hair."

"You think you know something?" Sal laughed. "You don't got proof of nothing."

"Sure we do," I bluffed, feeling my eyelid betray me and begin to twitch. "Matt isn't the only person who saw you at Perry's. We can place you at Perry's and The Wharf Hotel."

I didn't break eye contact with him, even though the last location was a guess on my part. I figured he must have been at his wife's styled shoot when the police arrived to question Antonio. I recognized him as the man I hadn't known at her styled shoot on the rooftop, so it wasn't a stretch to guess he was at her other styled shoot.

His dark eyes flashed with anger. "So? I got business dealings with the owner of Perry's, and I go to all my wife's events to keep people in line."

"I'll bet it works," muttered Kate.

"So what happened?" I asked, pushing Kate behind me as I backed toward the door. "Your wife got mad at Cher Noble and you took care of it? But you had to take care of Blanche Davidian, the witness who was leaving the crime scene at the same time you were and might have been able to finger you for the murder?"

I could hear Kate and Fern shuffling backward, but I didn't want to look at them and give them away. "So when Antonio was picked up, you had to kill him before he talked to the cops because he might have seen you at Perry's, right?"

Sal opened and closed his fists. "You got it all wrong, girlie. I just want to set your friend straight."

"I don't think so." I twisted around to face Kate and Fern. "Run for it!"

Fern threw open the glass door and ran out with Kate close at his heels. I held tight to Hermes while I dashed out with them, hearing Matt scream over the furious yelping coming from the dog under my arm and Sal curse and scramble to chase after us.

Fern looked over his shoulder and shrieked, throwing his arms up as he darted around the cocktail tables. I was afraid to look behind me, but I could hear heavy breathing and Matt yelling for me to get out of his way.

"Watch out, Annabelle!" Fern called out as he craned his neck to look at me.

Kate glanced back, her eyes wide as she stumbled and knocked into Fern, who teetered for a moment on the edge of the pool before falling in. I heard a splash behind me and realized Sal had jumped in after Fern and was trying to swim to him, a murderous look on his face.

"He's going to drown him," Kate yelled to me.

I searched the pool area for something to use as a weapon but came up short. Fern let out a piercing scream when he saw Sal coming for him and started flailing in the water as he tried to make it to the side.

The pink-and-white-striped pole in the center of the pool swayed as Sal knocked into it. I knew it had taken hours for the crew to set up the poles and draping, but I couldn't let this guy kill Fern. I reached for the closest pole along the edge of the pool and pulled it out of the clamps holding it steady, before kicking off my flats and jumping into the pool.

The freezing water was a shock, and my teeth began chattering immediately. I wiped the water from my eyes and located

Fern. He was a few feet away from a ladder with Sal almost on top of him. My pole still had pink fabric attached to the top, but I managed to slam it down in front of Sal, startling him.

He turned his attention to me, cutting through the water in my direction. I lifted my pole and brought it down again, missing his head by inches. He roared as he lunged for me, taking hold of my pole and jerking it toward him. I lost my grip and let go, backing away from him and treading water as the pool floor dropped off under me.

"Right behind you," Kate cried, flinging off her heels and pulling down another pole before landing with a splash next to me.

Before Kate could raise her pole, Sal grabbed it and pulled it out of her arms. At this point I could hear shouting and barking from the pool deck, but it was hard to see through all the fabric now sagging around us.

"Swim, Kate!" I called out as I turned and began cutting through the water.

I reached the side and tried to hoist myself up when I felt a hand pull me back by my ponytail. I went under, my arms reaching back and trying to loosen the iron grip on my hair as he held me under. The shouts from around the pool were muffled under the water as I scratched at his hands and arms. As my lungs began to burn, I felt a massive surge of water knocking me forward. The grip on my hair released, and I pushed up to the surface.

A pair of arms pulled me out of the pool, and I was standing next to a dripping wet Fern who patted me on the back as I coughed up water. I turned around and saw both Buster and Mack in the water, holding Sal limply between them.

"They landed on him," Fern said. "Both of them."

The two enormous men jumping in must have been the surge of water I felt. I was a little surprised there was any water left inside the pool at all.

"The draping!" Richard ran around the corner of the house, skidding to a stop when he saw Buster and Mack dragging Sal out of the pool, while Fern and I helped Kate up the ladder at the far end. "Are you all out of your minds? What are you doing in the pool?"

I pointed to the inert Sal as Buster and Mack deposited him on the concrete and Hermes circled him barking. "He's the killer."

Reese stepped out of the house, followed by Darla with half of her head in hot rollers and a Bloody Mary still in her hand, her mouth dangling open, and her celery stick nearly falling out.

Reese paused as he took in the chaotic scene, and his eyes lingered on my dripping wet form. "Who did you say was a killer?"

Kate, Fern, and I all pointed to the wet lump on the ground that was Sal. I wondered if we should check to see if he was breathing before I remembered him holding my head under water, and my concern vanished.

"Don't worry," Buster said, poking Sal with his toe. "He's not going anywhere."

The leather of Mack's vest groaned as he crossed his arms.

"Thanks, guys." I took a few steps over to the closest chaise lounge chair and sank onto it. "That's Tina Pink's husband. He killed Cher, Blanche, and Antonio."

Reese's eyebrows popped up.

"And he tried to drown Annabelle when she jumped in to save me," Fern said, his pink-and-white-striped vest clinging to his nearly transparent shirt as he sat down next to me. I looked into the pool and saw his straw hat floating in a corner.

"Then we jumped in," Mack said.

"And landed smack dab on top of Sal." Fern shook his head. "Seeing those two flying through the air was—"

"Terrifying," Kate finished for him.

Reese called for backup, slipped his phone into his jeans pocket, and sat beside me. He wrapped an arm around my shoulders. "How did you manage to get in this much trouble in the time it took me to drive over here?"

"We solved your case for you, Detective," Kate said. "Don't look a gift whore in the mouth."

Reese blinked a few times, and I could tell he was trying not to laugh. "Now that's advice you don't get every day."

Richard slapped a hand to his forehead. "Just shoot me."

CHAPTER 30

"I didn't think there would be this many cops to haul away one guy." Fern stood by the kitchen windows in a white terry cloth bathrobe and a towel turban on his head, both courtesy of Darla.

I adjusted my own robe—a fluffy pink one left in Debbie's old bedroom—as we watched Reese outside with the swarm of cops and other uniformed officials who'd descended on the backyard. "We didn't know Sal had been under investigation by the DEA for over a year."

"Talk about a surprise," Kate said as she perched on a barstool with her legs crossed and plenty of thigh showing underneath the red silk shorty robe she'd chosen from Darla's offerings.

"He was a nightclub owner, sweetie. Not a missionary." Fern ran his fingers through his wet hair. "I don't think anyone's surprised a guy like him ran drugs through his clubs."

We'd moved into the kitchen and shed our soaking wet clothes once the police had arrived in force. Now we were waiting to be questioned and for everyone to leave so we could clean up and continue with setup for Debbie's baby shower. Matt, aka Rhoda

Dendron, had disappeared in all the confusion, although I didn't blame him.

"Are you sure we shouldn't postpone?" Darla asked Richard as they walked into the kitchen.

"Absolutely not." Richard shifted Hermes from one hip to the other. "Give us a few hours and you'll never know the police were here."

Darla picked up a coffee pot from the counter. "Can I freshen anyone's coffee?"

Darla had made coffee to warm us all up, but I'd noticed her topping off the pot with Irish whiskey before she served it. I looked at my mostly untouched cup and shook my head. I didn't think being tipsy when I spoke with the police was the best plan.

Fern left his post at the window to walk over, holding out his oversized mug. "Just a splash, hon."

"Thank you for the robes," I said to Darla.

"Don't mention it. I couldn't have you sitting around in wet clothes." She filled her own mug to the brim. "I only wish I'd had robes big enough for Buster and Mack."

I looked out to the pool deck where their enormous black leather pants and vests were drying in the sun.

"Where are they?" Kate asked.

"Upstairs going through my selection of California king sheets and blankets to see what works," Darla said. "Although I don't know how they're going to ride home on their bikes in them."

I eyed the drying leather clothes and noticed they were beginning to pucker. Somehow I didn't think they'd be squeezing themselves into those pants anytime soon.

"Where is she?" The shrill female voice from the front of the house made us all jump.

"Who is that?" Darla asked, spinning around.

Kate looked at me as we heard the front door slam, her brows pressed together to form a crease between her eyes. "You don't think . . . ?"

Richard led the way to the foyer where Tina Pink stood, her face red and her eyes bulging.

"You got my husband arrested." Her eyes moved from Richard to Kate to Fern and to me as she spoke. "This is all your fault."

"Actually, this is your fault." Fern wrapped his hands around his mug and took a sip, seemingly unperturbed by Tina's outburst. "He knocked off Cher because you wanted him to, which I think makes you an accessory to murder. Am I right?"

Richard put a hand on his hip and gave a dismissive sniff while Hermes yipped in Tina's direction. "That's what it sounds like to me, too."

Tina glared at me and stamped her foot. "I have no idea what you're talking about. She looked around as if searching for something, her gaze darting from person to person until she fixed on the carousel. "You all think you're so smart, don't you? Well, this is what I think of you and your friends."

She swung a foot out to the side and karate kicked the horse closest to her, sending flower petals flying and denting the horse's side.

Kate gasped and put both hands over her mouth, and I heard myself suck in air. Hermes let out a torrent of barks and tried to get out of Richard's arms.

Tina grinned and lifted her foot again but was stopped by a thundering noise as both Buster and Mack descended the stairs with giant sheets flapping and billowing in their wake. They sounded like a herd of buffalo and looked like plus-sized ghosts. Tina screamed and backed up against the front door.

When Buster and Mack came to a stop at the bottom of the stairs, I got a good look at what they were wearing. Mack had fashioned himself a toga out of lavender monogrammed sheets with the embroidered 'D' emblazoned on his chest. Buster, on the other hand, had tied a brightly colored floral sheet around his waist and used a matching one as a cape.

LAURA DURHAM

"I wouldn't do that if I were you," Buster said, his voice a low rumble as he tossed one end of his floral cape over his shoulder.

"I think it's someone's turn to talk to the police." Mack took Tina by the arm, and Hermes yipped in agreement.

As Buster and Mack marched her out the front door, Tina snapped her head in my direction. "This isn't over, Annabelle."

Richard patted my arm. "Don't worry, darling. She won't be able to do much damage to you where she's heading."

I couldn't help giving a little shudder. I hoped this was the last I'd be seeing of Tina Pink.

"We thought we heard your voices," Jesse said as he and Stefan leaned into the foyer through the open front door.

"What are you guys doing here?" Kate asked, walking over and giving Jesse a hug and Stefan an awkward pat on the arm.

"We live nearby and we were out on a walk. Stefan insists on us walking each day." Jesse appraised our robes. "Is everything okay?"

"It is now," I said. "The police arrested Tina Pink's husband for the murders."

Stefan raised a single eyebrow, but Jesse threw a hand over his mouth.

"Did he confess?" Jesse asked.

"No, but as soon as he regains consciousness, I'm sure he will." Kate pointed to me. "He tried to drown Annabelle five minutes ago."

"You poor thing." Jesse shook his head. "Is there anything we can do? It looks like you have enough bathrobes."

"We're fine," I said. "Thanks for asking."

"Actually, Annabelle." Stefan met my eyes. "Do you have a moment to talk?"

Jesse sighed. "Not this again. Ignore him, Annabelle. The wedding was wonderful, especially under the circumstances."

"No, it's fine." If I had to have it out with Stefan, I'd rather get it over with. Even if I was at a decided disadvantage by wearing a

212

bathrobe and having dripping wet hair. I jerked a thumb toward the study located off the foyer. "Why don't we duck in here?"

"Don't go too far," I said, catching Kate's arm as I passed.

"In these?" Kate asked, sweeping a hand down the front of her short red robe.

"How is the robe less revealing than anything you normally wear?" Richard muttered.

Kate assessed her outfit. "You may be right. With the right jewelry this could be a great dress."

Fern touched a hand to the red silk. "What it needs is a statement belt."

"What I need is an aspirin," I said.

"Don't worry about me," Richard mumbled as Kate pulled him and Fern away toward the kitchen. "I only suffered a minor heart attack, thank you very much."

Fern pushed his mug at Richard. "Have a drink. It helps."

"Just because I didn't jump in the pool, no one thinks I suffered," Richard said, his voice getting fainter as Kate pushed him down the hall.

"Why didn't you say so?" Fern said. "I can push you in the pool."

I tried to ignore Richard's grumbling punctuated by his dog's yipping as I held the door open for Stefan and followed him into the wood-paneled room lined with bookshelves on three sides.

He turned to face me, perching on the edge of the large mahogany desk. "I wanted to thank you."

I had the urge to shake my head to be sure I'd heard correctly. "I beg your pardon?"

"I don't think anyone else could have handled me and a murder the way you did." He reached into his pants pocket and pulled out an envelope. "This is a small thank you."

I took the envelope and could see the outline of a check inside, although I couldn't read the amount. "I don't know what to say. I didn't think you were happy."

He cracked a small smile. "I'm working on being happy. Jesse has insisted I spend more time at home, which is helping. Since I barely saw him during our engagement, I figure I owe him."

I returned his smile. "I wish you both the best."

The door behind us opened, and Jesse poked his head inside. "Do I get to thank her now?"

Stefan gave my arm a stiff pat as he left the room and Jesse came inside.

"So?" Jesse said. "Have you opened the check yet?"

I instinctively looked down at the envelope, but shook my head.

He winked at me. "Well, go on. I want to see what amount Stefan finally settled on."

I turned around and took a letter opener from the desk and sliced open the envelope. I glanced up as I felt Jesse behind me, no doubt angling for a better view of the check. My eyes caught his reflection in the glass of the large framed map over the desk, his arms reaching up and over my head as light glinted off something thin and shiny between his hands. I felt a burst of adrenaline as I realized the something was wire. I elbowed him as hard as I could in the ribs, diving to the side and rolling onto the carpet.

He grunted in pain and dropped the wire he'd been holding.

"You?" I scrambled to my feet and ran behind the desk since he was blocking my way to the door.

He snatched the wire from the floor, his hands covered by black leather gloves. "Sorry for the unpleasant surprise, honey."

"I don't get it. It was Sal."

He gave a quick jerk of his head. "No, and as soon as he's questioned you'll discover it wasn't him. You're much smarter than I gave you credit for, Annabelle. I knew if I gave you enough time, you'd have worked it out. Don't let anyone ever tell you wedding planning is for airheads."

"Thanks for the pep talk." I took a step to the side and bumped into the standing globe. "I don't get it. What reason did you have to kill any of those people?"

"Money, honey. Meaning Stefan's."

I scooted around the globe so it was between us. "What did Cher have to do with it?"

"I made the mistake of telling Cher about a few of my dalliances during one of the pre-marriage counseling sessions." Jesse pulled the wire taut between his hands, and I noticed his thick biceps flex. How had I not registered how muscular this guy was before now?

"Cher Noble did pre-marriage counseling?" I asked. "Was she trained?"

Jesse tilted his head at me. "That's exactly what Stefan asked. Cher was trying to be full-service, and I wanted to support her."

That would have been sweet if he wasn't confessing to her murder.

"Aren't those sessions something you do as a couple?" I asked, trying to keep my tone light and casual so he'd keep talking.

"Usually, but Stefan didn't show up. Not a shock. I was upset, and I spilled too much to Cher. Unfortunately, she decided she couldn't marry us unless I cleared the air with Stefan."

"And you didn't want to?"

Jesse laughed. "He would have left me and taken all his lovely money with him. I hadn't put up with his moods and demands for so long to lose it all when I was so close. I snuck out of the makeup room on Saturday and tried to talk to Cher, but she wouldn't back down."

"So you strangled her?"

"It wasn't planned. I saw some wire as well as a pair of gloves lying with the florist's supplies and got the idea. It was horrible, if you want to know the truth."

I took a few steps to my right and he mirrored my moves. "And Blanche?"

"She was storming out the first time I went into the library to talk to Cher. I couldn't be sure she wouldn't put two and two together, especially when I overheard her at Perry's and realized she was going to talk to the police."

I felt my stomach churn. So my having Blanche talk to the police did get her killed.

I gestured at the length of wire in his hands. "Is that the same wire?"

He gave a half shrug. "Call me a sentimental fool, but I've been carrying it around with me."

There were a lot of things I could think of calling him right now. A sentimental fool wasn't one of them. "Why kill Antonio? Were you on a roll?"

Jesse stamped a foot on the Persian carpet. "Do you think any of it was easy for me? I'm the nice one."

I might beg to differ. I slid my hand into the pocket of the robe and felt my phone. Without looking, I scanned my thumb. I cast a quick glance down as I tried to redial the last number I'd called and hoped Reese would answer.

"I saw the police escorting him out of The Wharf and heard them talking about taking him in for questioning about Blanche's murder. I remembered seeing him at Perry's. When I lowered the gold velvet, the flowers got bumped and he fixed them. I felt sure he could place me near the coffin. So when a car hit the patrol car he was in, I got him out of the backseat and told him I would help him escape. That one was as much luck as anything."

I felt like smacking myself on the forehead. Of course. Jesse and Stefan had been staying at The Wharf after the wedding since they couldn't leave for their honeymoon right away. "But instead of helping him you pushed him into the Potomac River in handcuffs?"

"I didn't want to." Jesse gave me a pleading smile and wrapped the wire around his gloved hands. "Like I don't want to kill you, but it does seem to get easier each time."

"That makes two of us who don't want you to kill me." I hoped my call had gone through and Reese was hearing all this, but there was an equal chance I'd opened my Facebook feed.

Jesse made a clucking noise and stepped closer to me. "Don't make this messy."

The door opened silently behind him, and I watched out of the corner of my eye as the muzzle of a gun appeared, followed by a hand, and finally Reese's entire arm.

"If I were you, I'd drop that," Reese said once he'd angled half his body inside the room.

Jesse spun around and dropped the wire in surprise, opening and closing his mouth. "It isn't what it looks like. Annabelle and I were having a friendly conversation."

"Lace your hands behind your head and get down on the ground," Reese told him.

Jesse began to cry as he lay on the floor and Reese cuffed him. I almost felt sorry for him, even though I knew he was guilty of multiple murders.

I followed Reese out into the foyer as he led Jesse to where a pair of uniformed officers waited for him. Stefan's expression was stony as he watched Jesse being taken out the front door sobbing.

I ran back into the study and searched the floor for the envelope I'd dropped when I'd been evading a killer. I picked up the check and flipped it over, almost staggering back when I saw the amount. A two thousand dollar tip didn't make up for almost being strangled, but it was a start.

"Are you okay?" Reese asked from the door.

I tucked the check into the pocket of the robe. "I'm okay. I'm glad you got my call."

"Me too." He crossed the room and pulled me into a hug. "Your friends are chomping at the bit to see you, but I wanted a moment alone first."

"I'm surprised they were cool with that."

He grinned. "I do have a gun."

I laughed. "So what happens to Sal? He still tried to drown me."

"It looks like he's going to cut a deal by working with the DEA to nab the top guy in a pretty large drug smuggling operation." Reese brushed a wet strand of hair out of my eyes. "Don't worry. We have enough on this guy already to put him away for a few years. And now we have enough on your groom to put him away for a few lifetimes."

I let out a breath and felt my shoulders relax. "At least he won't kill anyone else."

Reese's face became serious. "I'm glad you're safe, but about you staying out of trouble . . ."

"I swear I didn't have any idea I'd end up having encounters with two deranged men when I came to work today," I said, watching his mouth pull up into a half smile.

"I know." He cupped my chin in his hand. "I think maybe I haven't been doing a good enough job keeping you out of trouble. I haven't been able to keep an eye on you like I want to."

I tilted my head at him. "It's not like you can post a twenty-four-hour guard outside my apartment."

"Not outside." He leaned down and kissed me lightly, his lips soft against mine.

Even though the kiss was gentle, I felt my fingers tingle. I pressed one hand against his chest to keep myself steady.

He kissed me again, this time deeper, his arm around my waist pulling me tight against him. When he pulled away, he whispered in my ear, "I had a different idea. It involves us being together much more."

Even though my head felt fuzzy, one thought registered faintly in the depths of my brain. Richard was not going to like this.

The End

(For a sneak peek at the next book in the series, continue reading!)

FREE DOWNLOAD!

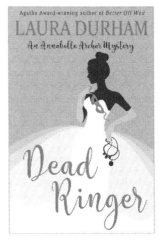

A GLAMOROUS BRIDAL SHOW.
A CLEVER JEWELRY HEIST.

CAN ANNABELLE TRACK
DOWN THE BAUBLES AND
NAB A BURGLAR?

amazonkindle

nook

kobo

 iBooks

Get your free copy of the novella "Dead Ringer"
when you sign up to the author's mailing list.

Get started here:

deadringer.lauradurham.com

SNEAK PEEK OF BOOK 9: WED OR ALIVE

Chapter One

I stood underneath the high-peaked tent and gazed past the rows of wooden folding chairs across the lush green lawn. The massive house—built to resemble a Tuscan villa—sat at the top of the gentle grass slope. A long pool stretched out from its patio, adorned with a statue of a Roman goddess at the far end of the blue water. The white marble goddess already wore a floral wreath, evidence that my floral team had begun the pool area decor. I took my wedding day schedule from the pocket of my black dress and checked that off the timeline.

Tucking a long strand of auburn hair back into my bun, I raised my face to one of the fans tucked high in the corners of the tent, but I felt the warm air barely stir. I would need to turn the fans to high before the two hundred plus wedding guests arrived and filled the tent. Even though the ceremony programs were printed to resemble old-fashioned paper fans used in country churches, I suspected they would be of little help in the June heat.

Two black-and-white clad figures waddled toward me from the house, their arms flapping at their side to help them keep their balance and their heads bobbing back and forth. I glanced down at my timeline again and put a check mark next to the line that read, "Penguins arrive."

"Down here." I waved my arms in the air so the handler could see me as I stepped out from under the tent to meet her.

The penguins came to a stop in front of me, and I fought the urge to pet them, reminding myself they were wild animals even though they looked adorable.

"I'm Annabelle Archer with Wedding Belles. The wedding planner." I extended my hand to the short-haired woman in jeans accompanying the penguins. "I think we spoke on the phone."

The woman shook my hand. "I know I'm a little early but I wanted to give myself time to find this place."

"It's a bit outside the city." I cast my eyes over the sprawling estate with its wrought-iron gate, stately driveway lined with tall Italian cypress trees, and horse stables complete with rolling fields. It even smelled like we were far away from the city with the scent of cut grass—and the faintest trace of horse manure—in the air. "But look at the upside. There's tons of free parking."

She chuckled. "True. It's better than hunting for a space in downtown DC."

"Before I forget to tell you, the bride decided against having the penguins carry the rings down the aisle." I didn't mention that I'd spent hours talking her out of this. After a bad experience with a pair of dogs running off with the wedding rings, I'd adopted a "no animals carrying expensive jewelry" policy.

"So just the photo shoot with the couple and mingling during cocktail hour?"

"You got it. We still have a couple of hours until go time, so why don't you hang out in the house?" As if they heard me, the penguins turned and started waddling away. "I doubt your little guys like the heat."

"I think they're heading for the pool."

I personally didn't have a problem with the penguins taking a dip. "It's salt-water. I think it's safe."

My assistant, Kate, did a double-take as she passed the penguins on her way down the hill, stumbling a bit in her heels and catching herself before she tumbled the rest of the way.

"I forgot about the penguins," she said when she reached me.

I tapped my schedule.

"I know, I know." She flicked a hand through her blond bob. "I didn't have time to memorize it yet, General."

"Another date with the naval officer?" I asked, ducking back under the tent to avoid the sun.

She frowned. "He's been deployed. No, last night's date was with a lawyer who works at Langley."

I tucked my schedule back into my pocket. "He's a lawyer for the CIA?"

She put a finger to her lips and shot a glance over her shoulder. "I can't talk about it."

"You know he isn't a spy, right?" I said. "They don't send lawyers to infiltrate terrorist cells."

"We don't know that. What would be more of a surprise than a bunch of buttoned-up lawyers busting out the spy moves?"

"Not much," I admitted.

"Enough about my love life." Kate nudged me. "I want to hear the latest on yours."

I hoped my impending heat stroke hid the blush I felt at the mention of my love life. After a rocky start and a bit of on-again off-again action, I'd been dating DC detective Mike Reese steadily for several months. Things still weren't smooth sailing since we both had crazy work schedules—especially since I was in the thick of my busy season—and not all my friends were as crazy about Reese as Kate was. My best friend, Richard, had been giving the relationship the cold shoulder since he'd decided my dating Reese meant he spent less time with me.

"Fine," I said. "Everything's fine."

"Fine?" Kate tapped her foot on the grass. "That tells me nothing. Have you decided yet?"

I avoided her eyes. "I've been too busy to give it much thought."

"If a smoking hot cop asked me to move in together, I wouldn't take a month to tell him yes."

"It's complicated," I said.

She tilted her head at me. "You mean Richard?"

"And work. We *have* been very busy."

Kate took my hands in hers. "Unless Richard plans to keep you warm at night, I don't think he should have a vote. This is your life after all."

I squeezed Kate's hands. "I know, but Richard has been my best friend since I moved to DC. It's hard to see this come between us."

"He'll get over it." Kate dropped my hands. "He may fast in protest for a while—or maybe cut out truffles—but he'll survive."

My hesitation had more to do with my best friend, but it was hard to admit that I was just as much afraid of my life changing as Richard was. I cleared my throat. "How's the bride doing upstairs?"

"Good. She's a little nervous so Fern's calming her down with his patented blend of charm and dirty jokes."

"As long as he's not getting the bridal party drunk," I said.

Kate hesitated. "Would you be okay with tipsy?"

I let out a deep sigh. "Are we talking him or the bride?"

Kate bobbled her head, which I did not take as a good sign.

"Hallelujah." She threw her arms in the air as she spotted the lemonade station on the other side of the tent. "I'm dying of thirst. The only thing to drink in the house is champagne." She held up a hand before I could speak. "And you know I follow your rule about not drinking alcohol at weddings."

I followed her over to the rustic wooden table with the two large glass beverage dispensers, one filled with traditional lemonade and one filled with raspberry lemonade—indicated by painted wooden signs hanging around the glass containers.

Kate took a champagne flute, filled it with plain lemonade and handed it to me before filling her own. "No Mason jars?" she teased, knowing my aversion to the rustic wedding trend.

"Not on my watch." I took a sip and felt several degrees cooler as I swallowed the sweet drink.

"As I suspected," Richard said as he strode down the hill toward us, his beige blazer flapping. "You two are drinking on the job while I'm slaving away in the kitchen."

Kate downed her glass and refilled it. "How is it you never break a sweat when you slave away?"

I'd often wondered the same thing. Richard, owner of the renowned Richard Gerard Catering and my best friend, had a talent for remaining spotless no matter the temperature or disaster.

"It's a lot of work to direct my staff and manage the load-in." Richard smoothed the front of his linen blend jacket. "Just because I don't personally haul boxes, does not mean I'm not working hard." He took out a small mister and sprayed his face with—from what I could tell from the few drops that flew into my face —rose water.

"Of course it doesn't." I touched a hand to his arm, hoping to mollify him. We didn't need Richard worked up this early in an event. "Would you like some lemonade?"

He eyed the glass jars. "Perhaps a drop. The sun is relentless."

June in the Washington DC area could be mild or it could be sweltering. Unfortunately, on this wedding day, we'd drawn the short straw.

Kate handed him a glass. "Bottoms up."

Richard took a sip and dabbed his mouth with one of the linen cocktail napkins fanned out on the table. "So refreshing." He set the empty glass on the table and put one hand on his hip. "You didn't tell me we were having an armed militia attend the wedding."

"What?" I blinked at him a few times before snapping my fingers. "You mean the father-of-the-bride's personal security detail?"

Richard pointed to a man in all black walking the perimeter of the patio. "There are at least half a dozen of these guys and they're all packing serious heat."

Kate winked at him. "You sound so butch when you talk like that."

Richard ignored her. "Isn't this excessive for a guy who owns a pharmaceutical company?"

"It's not just any pharma company." I dropped my voice. "They got a major contract with DOD last year. Very hush-hush."

"Department of Defense?" Kate asked. "What does a drug manufacturing company have to do with defense?"

I wasn't surprised Kate knew the acronym off the top of her head. She'd dated men at every major government department and knew all the abbreviations by now.

"And how do you know this?" Richard asked.

"You told me I should Google my clients," I said.

Richard beamed at me. "Look at you doing research on your clients. I'm so proud. I hope you charged them more when you found out."

I headed out of the tent, gesturing for Richard and Kate to follow me. "You know I don't raise my prices just because someone is wealthy."

He let out an exasperated breath. "Still so much to learn, darling."

"Anyway," I said, letting Kate lean on me as we walked up the hill and her heels got stuck in the grass. "I figure the contract must be top secret. Why else would he have guards following him everywhere? You don't do that if you're manufacturing ADD meds."

Richard paled under his bronzer. "That's a scary thought. You don't think we're in danger, do you?"

"Kate and I have been coming to the house for six months and we've never seen anything out of the ordinary, right?" I stepped onto the paving stones of the pool deck and waited for Kate to pull her shoes out of the ground.

She scrunched her mouth to one side. "I do see a pair of penguins swimming in the pool."

Richard held up his palms as we watched the pair of animals splash in the water. "Don't get me started on the penguins. You know my feelings about livestock at weddings, Annabelle."

"Penguins are hardly livestock. You should be grateful I talked them out of the llamas."

"Llamas? They must be out of their minds." Richard looked heavenward. "I used to think it was absurd to have dogs in weddings. Now I long for the days when a cocker spaniel was the worst of our worries."

I stepped back as one of penguins slapped his flipper, sending droplets of water onto the pool deck.

"Watch it," Richard called out to the penguin, pointing to his shoes. "These are suede."

"I don't think he heard you," Kate said. "He's underwater."

"There you are." Fern stepped out one of the French doors to the house. "I need a little assistance."

His dark hair was pulled into a tight man bun at the top of his head but it was the crease between his eyebrows I noticed. "What's wrong? Please tell me another bride isn't passed out cold."

"Of course not, sweetie," Fern said, as if this had never happened to him before. "But she says to cancel the wedding and send everyone home. She's changed her mind about getting married."

To be continued . . .

(To order **Wed or Alive**, turn the page.)

ALSO BY LAURA DURHAM

Read the entire Annabelle Archer Series in order:

Better Off Wed

For Better Or Hearse

Dead Ringer

Review To A Kill

Death On The Aisle

Night of the Living Wed

Eat, Prey, Love

Groomed For Murder

Wed or Alive

To Love and To Perish

To get notices whenever I release a new book, follow me on BookBub:

https://www.bookbub.com/profile/laura-durham

Did you enjoy this book? You can make a big difference!

I'm extremely lucky to have a loyal bunch of readers, and honest reviews are the best way to help bring my books to the attention of new readers.

If you enjoyed *Groomed for Murder*, I would be forever grateful if you could spend two minutes leaving a review (it can be as short as you like) on Goodreads, Bookbub, or your favorite retailer.

Thanks for reading and reviewing!

For Ric Marino and Monte Durham,
dear friends and constant inspiration.
Richard and Fern have nothing on
their real-life counterparts!

ACKNOWLEDGMENTS

A huge thank you to all of my wonderful readers, especially my beta readers and my review team. You are all amazing and so appreciated! A special shout-out to the beta readers who catch all my goofs and let me know if something doesn't make sense before the book goes to print: Linda Reachill, Sheila Kraemer, Jan Scholefield, Linda Fore, Annemarie Esposito, Wendy Green, Vivian Shane, Charlene Eshleman, Sandra Anderson, Katherine Munro, Sharon Thach, Tony Noice, Barb Foerst, Karen Diamond, Lisa Hudson, Nicole Drake, and Bill Saunders. You all have eagle eyes! And thank you to everyone who leaves reviews. They really make a difference, and I am grateful for every one of them!

Thank you to my editor, Sandy Chance, whose work is fast and fabulous, and to my cover designer, Keri Knutson, who created the new look of the Annabelle books (which I adore).

A virtual hug to Bill Saunders who suggested I feature a gay wedding in my next book (a great idea). I'm always open to reader suggestions, so if you have ideas for a future book or something you'd like to see, let me know!

ABOUT THE AUTHOR

Laura Durham has been writing for as long as she can remember and has been plotting murders since she began planning weddings over twenty years ago in Washington, DC. Her first novel, BETTER OFF WED, won the Agatha Award for Best First Novel.

When she isn't writing or wrangling brides, Laura loves traveling with her family, standup paddling, perfecting the perfect brownie recipe, and reading obsessively.

She loves hearing from readers and she would love to hear from you! Send an email or connect on Facebook, Instagram, or Twitter (click the icons below).

Find me on:
www.lauradurham.com
laura@lauradurham.com

Made in the USA
Columbia, SC
18 September 2023

23036261R00145